Masterji and Other Stories

OTHER LOTUS TITLES

AMRITA PRITAM	*The Other Dimension*
ARJAN SINGH	*Arjan Singh's TigerBook*
DHANANAJAYA SINGH	*The House of Marwar*
E. JAIWANT PAUL	*'By My Sword and Shield'*
E. JAIWANT PAUL	*Rani of Jhansi: Lakshmi Bai*
GANESH SAILI	*Glorious Garhwal*
GERALDINE FORBES (ed.)	*The Memoirs of Dr. Haimabati Sen*
INDIRA MENON	*The Madras Quartet*
IRADJ AMINI	*Koh-i-noor*
J.C. WADHAWAN	*Manto Naama*
JOHN LALL	*Begam Samru*
JYOTI JAFA	*Nurjahan*
KHUSHWANT SINGH	*Kipling's India*
KANWALBIR PUSHPENDRA SINGH	*The Ruse*
K. M. GEORGE	*The Best of Thakazhi Sivasankara Pillai*
LAKSHMI SUBRAMANIAN	*Medieval Seafarers*
LALI CHATTERJEE	*Muonic Rhapsody and Other Encounters*
MAGGI LIDCHI-GRASSI	*Great Golden Legend of the Mahabharata*
MANOHAR MALGONKAR	*Dropping Names*
MUSHIRUL HASAN	*India Partitioned.* 2 vols
MUSHIRUL HASAN	*Educational Institutions in India*
NAMITA GOKHALE	*Mountain Echoes*
NINA EPTON	*Mumtaz Mahal: Beloved Empress*
P. LAL	*The Bhagavad Gita*
ROMESH BHANDARI	*Goa*
RUSKIN BOND	*Ruskin Bond's Green Book*
SHOVANA NARAYAN	*Rhythmic Echoes and Reflections: Kathak*
SUDHIR KAKAR (ed.)	*Indian Love Stories*
VIBHUTI NARAIN RAI	*Curfew in the City*
V. S. NARAVANE	*Best Stories from the Indian Classics*
V. S. NARAVANE (ed.)	*Devdas and Other Stories by Sarat Chandra*

FORTHCOMING TITLES

CLAUDIA PRECKEL	*Begums of Bhopal*
JYOTI JAFA	*Really Your Highness*
MUSHIRUL HASAN	*From John Company to the Indian Republic*
RALPH RUSSELL	*Ghalib*
V.G.KIERNAN	*Poems by Faiz*

Masterji and Other Stories

Maura Moynihan

LOTUS COLLECTION
ROLI BOOKS

Lotus Collection

This edition first published in 1999
Second Impression 2000
The Lotus Collection
An imprint of
Roli Books Pvt Ltd
M-75, G.K. II Market
New Delhi 110 048
Phones: 6442271, 6462782, 6460886
Fax: 6467185, 6213978
E-mail: roli@vsnl.com
Website: rolibooks.com
Also at
Varanasi, Agra, Jaipur and the Netherlands

Cover painting and line sketches by Maura Moynihan
Back cover: Photo by Tsering Rhitar

ISBN: 81-7436-071-9
Rs. 195

Typeset in Galliard by Roli Books Pvt Ltd and
printed at Pritha Offsets Pvt Ltd, New Delhi-110 028

For my mother and father
who gave me India.

"Was it a vision, or a waking dream?
Fled is that music:—do I wake or sleep?"

John Keats

‘I am a refugee from the new world
seeking asylum in the old world
of immutable truths,
seeking to turn the Wheel of Dharma.
In the new world we were told
that machines would deliver us from slavery
that this new order would make us free,
as we were delivered to industrial servitude,
made free to plunder whatever’s here,
free to waste our liberty in spurious cheer.
Nature is violated, displaced
We live hardened to Her pain, have
chosen disavowal, disgrace. . . .
We meet, drenched in evening rain
worlds apart, here we are the same.’

Maura Moynihan

Contents

Samsara. The illusions and turmoil of Samsara (the beginningless cycle of repeated births in this world), which is like a wild and dangerous ocean into which we endlessly incarnate. Numerous forms like Yidam, dakini, Naga, yogini and Maya (the illusory reality) prevent us from recognizing the true nature of the Universe.

High Commissioner for Refugees

LEYTON HAD JUST BEEN POSTED TO DELHI AS the United Nations High Commissioner for Refugees for South Asia. Davis was on vacation. The two had been freshman year room-mates at Princeton, and the college tie still bound them, though Leyton couldn't stand travelling with Davis. Davis assumed that every cab driver, waiter and shopkeeper was a thief, and the smallest transaction turned into a fight. Leyton thought it was undignified of Davis to argue over two dollars with someone half his body weight and made the point after Davis spent fifteen minutes screaming at a *chaiwalla* at the Sikkim-West Bengal border. When they arrived in Gangtok, Leyton quickly paid the driver while Davis fussed with his camera equipment.

25.3.93: Gangtok, Sikkim. Flew from Delhi to Bhagdogra, took a taxi to Gangtok, followed the Tista river, its turquoise water, white sandy banks, ferns, bamboo, banana. Some slash and burn, sparse population, but not as badly deforested as Nepal. Stopped twice for Gold Spots and peanuts. Everyone speaks Hindi. Davis not annoyingly combative with the natives yet.

Banners everywhere welcoming His Holiness, the Dalai Lama.

Gangtok is unspectacular, though no children with distended stomachs and lice-ridden hair, flies crawling on their eyes; no beggars and lepers. Still, plenty of open sewers and a lot of the plainly offensive new architecture. Streets full of pilgrims: Bhutanese, Nepalis, Tibetans, Bengalis, the odd hippie, apparently here to see the Dalai Lama. Davis annoys, though I must give him credit for finding the guest house, a genuine Sikkimese home. Very charming. Davis complains about the food, as ever. I think it's fine. Can't get through to Delhi, none of the phones are working.

Pema, the owner of the guest house, invited Davis and Leyton to his room for tea. The brew was weak and tepid. Leyton saw Davis's lip curl, and quickly started asking questions.

"What's the Dalai Lama doing in Gangtok?"

"He's giving the Kalachakra Puja."

"Kala what?" Davis's eyebrows peeked over the edges of his reflector shades.

"It's a Buddhist teaching and initiation ceremony. That's why all the hotels and restaurants are full."

"What's the turnout?" asked Leyton.

"I hear it's about 80,000. I haven't been down to see it, I have to work."

"How many Tibetans?"

"Maybe five or six thousand. The Indian border guards turned away 40,000 for not having the proper permits. It's a regulation they rarely enforce, but this is a sensitive area as far as relations with China are concerned, so they enforced it at the last minute. My brother-in-law built a camp for 20,000 pilgrims, all the tents are empty. You should go down and see the puja some afternoon."

"Nah." Davis yawned without covering his mouth and pushed his chair away from the table. "I'm here to do some trekking."

"I'll arrange it for you. The two of you?"

"Come on, Leyton, get off your ass for once, you need it."

"If the phones are still down tomorrow I'll go for a drive."

26.3.93: No word on travel permits, so joined Davis on a tour of the valley. Our driver, a pliant, pleasant teenager, nevertheless forgot (or says he forgot) to fill the gas tank before we started out. Had to stop in Phodong to hunt for gas, we waited forty-five minutes at a tea shop. Poster of Christie Brinkley in a bikini above the cash register. Davis insisted we replace a ripped back tire. Driver kept resisting, till we almost keeled in a ravine. Wouldn't take us past Phodong, said it was a restricted area. I kept showing our papers (which didn't have permits but looked official) but to no avail. No visible signs of malnutrition among the villagers, no distended stomachs, but some hair discolour.

Visited a monastery. Beautiful frescoes, one image of a red female deity pouring a vermilion liquid from her vulva. Davis volubly amazed, I hastened to remind him that we were in a place of worship and should thus refrain from voicing opinion.

Davis went trekking the following day. Leyton stayed at the guest house writing in his journal and organising his files. He found a restaurant that sold the *Hindustan Times*, flown in from Calcutta. The place was decorated with a calendar from Vijay Opticals with a picture of a naval tanker, an official portrait of an unctuously grinning Chief Minister Bhandari, whom Leyton initially mistook for a Hindi film villain, and an old photograph of the Dalai Lama. Leyton tried to read the paper, but his eyes kept turning towards the photograph of the Dalai Lama. It was a simple black and white photograph faded at the edges, yet it seemed to vibrate in its broken frame like an icon.

Leyton tried to focus on the newspaper, but again his gaze returned to the Dalai Lama. He remembered that the Tibetan leader was speaking to 80,000 people somewhere in Gangtok. It was foolish not to at least go look at what was happening. He paid for his tea and asked directions to the Kalachakra.

From the bazaar, a road led downwards far below the heart of the city. Thousands of pilgrims lined the road, sat on roof tops, in trees, hung over railings and balconies for a view of the Kalachakra. Women carried the children on their backs and laps; old men turned prayer wheels; teenagers dangled cowboy boots over railings; grandchildren gently led grandparents; monks, nuns, nomads, housewives, army officers, beggars and tourists all moved towards the soccer field where the Dalai Lama imparted the Buddha's teachings. Leyton made his way towards the large tent where the Dalai Lama sat on a raised gold chair and spoke into a microphone.

Leyton heard phrases of the English translation—put others before the self, cherish one's enemies, understand the nature of impermanence—but the sun was too strong, so he decided to go back to the guest house for a cold drink. When he passed the VIP section a Sikkimese soldier carrying a bayonet and prayer beads beckoned him in. Leyton balked, he didn't have a hat, or sunglasses, but the soldier beckoned again, so he followed the man to a seat between an Indian army officer and two Bhutanese women who were perspiring heavily in silk *kiras* and nylon stockings. The Dalai Lama leaned into the microphone and spoke rapidly in Tibetan, then nodded to the translator. The heat was fierce, Leyton's skin was pale and burned easily. He was about to leave when a cloud floated in front of the sun. The Bhutanese ladies folded their umbrellas and wiped kerchiefs over their brows and noses; the army officer removed his sunglasses and opened a book of Buddhist scriptures. The Dalai Lama looked directly at Leyton and smiled. Leyton blushed, embarrassed and proud.

27.3.93: Visited the Kalachakra. Quite a spectacle. Sun brutally hot. Extraordinary array of faces and costumes. About forty Westerners, press-pen half full of Buddhist monks. Wonder how many from Tibet. Davis exhausted after a long day of trekking, easier to be with.

At two-thirty in the morning Leyton felt someone prod his shoulder.

"Have you got a first aid kit?" Pema's hands were covered in blood. "My friend Tashi is haemorrhaging."

Leyton grabbed Davis' first aid kit and followed Pema to a small room next to the kitchen. A young Tibetan monk lay on a cot, blood streaming from his nose. Leyton handed him a cotton handkerchief while Pema searched through the first aid kit.

"Did he fall down?"

"No, he has this kind of internal haemorrhaging very often. He was tortured when he was in prison in Tibet."

"Should we call a doctor?"

"There's not much one can do when the bleeding starts."

The cook knelt by Tashi's bed and held out a bowl of warm milk. Pema sat up to drink; more blood spurted out of his nose. Leyton handed him another handkerchief. "Why was he in prison?"

"He sat in front of the Jokhang temple and raised the Tibetan flag. The Chinese arrested him immediately. They wanted him to give the names of other monks who were involved in the demonstration. When he refused they beat him with electric cattle prods and iron bars. Two guards held him down while six others kicked him. They left him in his cell for nine days without food, water or blankets, then they hung him by his thumbs for several hours a day. When he fainted from pain, they doused him with cold water and continued beating him. He lost the use of his left hand."

"What happened after that?"

"He spent three years in prison. When he got out he was afraid to go back to his monastery, so he fled to India. He says several of his friends died under torture."

After fifteen minutes Tashi was able to sit up without bleeding. Leyton saw several long scars on his neck, his left hand limp in his lap. He looked very young, he couldn't have been older than twenty-four.

"Why did he leave Tibet?"

"He wants the world to know the truth about the Chinese occupation. He says he doesn't hate the Chinese, he just wants them to stop what they are doing to his country. He wants to know about your job. I told him you work for the United Nations. Is that right, or is it your friend?"

"I'm in the UN. Davis works for a US Congressman."

Tashi pointed to the milk. Leyton helped him sit up to drink. Tashi smiled in thanks, Leyton smiled back weakly.

Leyton lay awake in his bed the rest of the night and saw, again and again, images of Tashi being beaten and suspended by his thumbs, lying unconscious in a torture cell, Tashi's limp hand, the scars on his body, his childlike smile. Three years of torture and imprisonment had somehow failed to corrupt him. Leyton was ashamed for still nurturing wounds from two failed love affairs and not getting into Harvard. His courage had never been tested, he had never made any effort to learn if he had any courage at all, whereas this young monk had survived an unimaginable ordeal with astonishing, inexplicable grace. He resented Tashi for it.

In 1959, 110,000 Tibetan refugees followed the Dalai Lama to India when the Chinese army invaded Tibet. A whole generation of Tibetan children have grown up in India. Must visit the Tibetan settlements in Himachal, Karnataka, make a report for Geneva.

Drove through the old royal grounds of the deposed (and now deceased) Choegyal. A poignant desolation about the place, Indian army trucks everywhere. The Sikkimese we've spoken with feel the Indian occupation is illegal. Problem began with the British; Nepali labourers were moved in to work in the tea plantations in the 19th century. Population is now 80 percent Nepali. Pema says there are now seven million Chinese in Tibet, six million Tibetans.

The next day Leyton went back to the Kalachakra. He did not go to the VIP section, he sat on the ground among the nomads and pilgrims, and listened carefully to the Dalai Lama's words. The Dalai Lama's voice, the heat and the brilliant colours put him into a trance. "... understand that everything is impermanent, at the moment of death, no wealth, no friend can save you. Only the dharma ... " He remembered the two workers from Amnesty International who had come to him with the testimony of Tibetan refugees in Dharamsala. The pattern of torture was just as Tashi had described: coerced confessions, beating with metal rods, electric batons, suspensions .... "... by cherishing your enemy you develop patience and compassion ..." Leyton had been taught to despise his enemy, that forgiveness was weakness; "... compassion is like a magic elixir that transforms the crudest substance into gold ... " Very soon, it seemed, five hours had passed. A purple dusk spread quickly through the sky. Groups of monks went through the crowd handing out stalks of dried grass. Leyton took the grass, and tapped the arm of a Tibetan lady whom he had overheard speaking English.

"Excuse me, what's this for?"

"You put the long one under your mattress, the short one under your pillow and pay attention to your dreams tonight."

"What kind of dreams should I have?"

"His Holiness will tell us tomorrow, just remember your dreams when you wake up." She smiled, and handed him a small package. "Take some *tsampa* to eat. For the walk back up the hill."

Leyton fumbled with the package, then looked up to say

thank you, but the woman had disappeared in the crush of nomads, monks, children and housewives. He walked slowly up the hill, compressed by *chubas*, knapsacks, hands turning prayer wheels, turquoise and coral stones hanging from earlobes and necks, long braids twined with red tassels, the smell of butter-tea, incense and perspiration.

Leyton had been raised on legends of Asia. His father was a diplomat, his grandfather had been a missionary in Shanghai. He had always assumed that he would continue this lineage, which was why he joined the UN, but he had never thought much about his motives, other than carrying on a family tradition. He assumed that he was doing important work, he supervised projects, wrote memos, but he rarely did what he was doing now, moving anonymously among the people he ostensibly served. He realised that he paid little attention to how they lived when they weren't in refugee camps.

Went back to Kalachakra today. Cannot deny the devotion these people have for the Dalai Lama. Remarkable to observe. But is non-violence practical? Gandhi used non-violence on the British, who understand the rule of law, the Communists don't. At the turn of the century Buddhism was one of the world's largest religions, though now most Buddhist cultures have been decimated by communism.

Leyton fell asleep with his diary open on his lap. At twelve-thirty he heard a knock. Rousing himself, he opened the door and saw Tashi and Pema in the hall.

"Oh God, are you alright?"

"Yes, thank you, Tashi's alright today."

"Would you like a drink? We've got Scotch."

"Tashi won't because he's a monk, I won't because I had hepatitis last year, but please, go ahead. Tashi wants to ask you something."

"Of course, of course, come in, and sit down."

"Five monks from Tashi's monastery were arrested last week. He says they are being severely tortured. He just heard this from a Tibetan who has come for the Kalachakra. Tashi says the UN Charter on Human Rights was smuggled into Tibet and translated into Tibetan; they read it in his monastery. He says that since you work for the United Nations you could help his friends."

"Of course, of course, but tell me exactly what he'd like me to do."

"He is hoping you could contact the American ambassadors in Beijing and at the United Nations and ask for the release of these monks. We have their names. They are all from Ganden Monastery, they are now in Drapchi prison in Lhasa."

Leyton opened his book and took notes. Both ambassadors were friends of his father's.

"Tashi wants you to meet the man who brought this information. We have to be careful because there are Chinese agents here to report on the Kalachakra."

"Do you have a safe place to meet?"

"You can come to the place where the man is staying. It isn't far from here."

"Of course I'll come. I want to help."

"Let's meet here tomorrow morning before the teachings and we'll take you to him."

Leyton noted the meeting in his book, looked up at Tashi who clutched his hand and smiled through tears.

"We're having dinner with the two Swiss girls I met trekking," Davis informed Leyton. Hey, what did you do with my first aid kit?"

"Pema has it. A friend of his was haemorrhaging very badly."

"What happened?"

"He spent three years in a Chinese prison."

"Hmm. Rough." Davis was, Leyton noted with disgust, a hulking carnivore with an ivy league education and little compassion.

"He asked me to contact the American Embassy in Beijing to help get five of his friends out of prison. I feel I ought to do something."

"Well, you can't, because the State Department goes along with the Chinese line that Tibet is a part of China, so the embassy won't do anything. China's also got a seat on the Security Council, so nothing will happen there. Come on, you know all this. Besides, there are bigger issues at stake, regional balance of power, trade, nuclear proliferation, right?"

"There are always larger issues at stake, but you have to respond when someone asks for your help."

"You can't help every refugee that comes through your door. Give the guy some money, or give him one of your sweaters."

Leyton rolled over on his side so he wouldn't have to watch Davis rearrange his cameras, sunglasses, thermoses and clocks. He remembered his father saying, "People are tortured in the Third World, that's just the way it is. You get one out, two go in." He'd visited refugee camps in Thailand and Cambodia, but had never stayed for more than three days. He wasn't a doctor, he reasoned, he had administrative responsibilities, but in truth he didn't stay for more than three days because the place was too harsh and too crowded. He remembered the relief and pleasure he felt when stepping into the shower at the Bangkok Hilton, ordering room service, lingering over book reviews in the *Herald Tribune*. At the time he felt he had earned it, but now he wondered if he was a coward.

Davis bullied his way through dinner with detailed boasts of mountaineering in Nepal and Peru. The Swiss girls nodded dumbly. Leyton concluded early on that they were the kind of world travellers upon whom the world had made a very small impression. The restaurant was filled with Indian tourists, Tibetan monks and American and European Buddhists. The combined effects of Davis' tedious monologues, laughter from other tables and the blinking coloured lights strung across the ceiling induced Leyton to drink several beers, which made Davis and the Swiss girls tolerable, and obliterated the images of Tashi that kept careening into his field of vision.

After dinner Leyton was fairly drunk. One of the Swiss girls was also very drunk, and kept giggling and dropping her purse in the gutter. Leyton tripped over a Nepali coolie and blacked out. When he regained consciousness, he clutched Davis' arm and struggled to his feet. The dirt, the odours and moisture, the shrill violins of Hindi film music and the swarms of people and animals suddenly repulsed him. Asia was too old and diseased, it was beyond rescue, that's just the way it was—you couldn't do much about it... you let one person out, two go in.... The streets smelled of decay, the air enveloped him like an infection. He pressed his hand over his mouth and ran.

Leyton was almost asleep when one of Davis' brutish, snores jolted him awake. He saw the *kushu* grass protruding from his backpack. He remembered what the woman had said at the Kalachakra, to lie on the grass and observe his dreams. He got up and put the grass under his mattress and pillow, just to be safe.

In his dreams he heard people howling and sobbing and saw a wasteland of corpses and skulls stretching across the entire continent of Asia. He awoke at four-thirty, gasping, and flushed the *kushu* grass down the toilet.

At breakfast, Leyton received a telegram about a meeting in Kathmandu the following week. He packed his bags, paid the bill, and deliberately neglected to leave word that he would not be able to meet Tashi and Pema. Leyton paced frantically across the drive, waiting for the taxi. He wanted to leave before Pema and Tashi arrived.

"We have to stop in the bazaar for a minute," said Davis. "You only gave me five minutes to pack, not that I mind getting out of here."

"We'll miss the flight."

"No we won't. I need mineral water, it'll just take a minute."

The driver stopped at a *chi* stall. Davis got out. Leyton heard someone call his name. His first instinct was to hide, but he turned to the window and saw Tashi running towards the car. Davis sat in the back and slammed the door. Leyton shouted at the driver to start moving. The car lurched into the street, Tashi waved and shouted after it.

Bade farewell to Gangtok, with a tinge of regret that we couldn't visit Pemayangste. Would've been nice to see the old monastery, supposed to have murals. Left Sikkim with images of prayer flags and glorious mountains. Another harrowing drive in a rickety taxi, but the driver did his best to get us to Bhagdogra in time. A surprisingly comfortable flight back to Delhi. I'm amazed anew at how Indian Airlines has improved. Excited about Kathmandu. Sikkim was, in truth, something of a disappointment. Would rather be in Bangkok. On that, more later.

A Good Job in Delhi

THE HOUSE WHERE HARI WORKED WAS IN THE centre of New Delhi, near a lot of government bungalows and embassy residences. Hari got the job through his father's cousin whose son-in-law was the driver. Every day Hari dusted the shelves, washed the floor, arranged whatever papers had accumulated on the tables. There wasn't much to do, his employers, the Calloways, never had parties. Hari had initially looked forward to wearing a white suit and proffering drinks on a silver tray, as did his cousin Ranjit who worked for the French Consul General, but that never happened. Once in a great while two or three people came for dinner or drinks, and when they did the Calloways paid no attention to the servants' clothes.

Mrs Calloway was a journalist for an English newspaper. She preferred Pakistan. She said people in Lahore gave better parties and "didn't talk from both sides of their mouths." Hari couldn't figure out what the husband did; he told dinner guests he was writing a book about the Punjab but he never went up to the library, neither did he use his typewriter. Hari knew this because it was his job to dust the library and the typewriter never came out from under its plastic dust cover and there was never any paper in the wastebasket. From what Hari observed, Mr Calloway spent most of his time reading magazines and eating grilled cheese sandwiches on the *bersati*.

Hari lived in the dormitory behind the house with the other servants—a *chowkidar*, a dhobi, and Harmeet the cook. Over the years Harmeet had worked for various embassies and high commissions, and thus claimed to speak Italian, French, Danish and "Brazilian," which he had putatively studied during his four-year tenure at the Brazilian Embassy. One night the Calloways had a Brazilian demographer to dinner. They summoned Harmeet from the kitchen so the two could have a conversation. Hari watched from the doorway. He knew Harmeet didn't understand what the man was saying, but Harmeet invented a story line which was well received by the guest. When Harmeet was finally released, he ran into the kitchen, sweat streaming down his forehead, and yelled at Hari to get the dessert trays ready.

Harmeet was willfully obsequious in the Calloways' presence, but when alone with the other servants, he recounted calumnious tales of Mr Calloway's sexual habits. Hari consequently studied his employer with fierce curiosity, but the only noticeably peculiar thing Mr Calloway ever did was to entertain a middle-aged Australian woman when Mrs Calloway was out of town. Harmeet muttered about what they did when they were alone, but as far as Hari could see nothing much went on; they sat in the living room, smoked cigarettes and drank whiskey sodas. The woman always left promptly at 12.30 p.m. Mr Calloway turned out the lights in the living room, locked the front door and went to bed. It was strange that the woman never came when Mrs Calloway was there, but it was also strange that Mrs Calloway was always travelling. Hari soon gave up speculating about Mr Calloway's private life, and concentrated on pilfering chocolates and liqueurs, fishing European magazines out of the trash, and staying up late reading and eating in his room.

After Hari got the job in Delhi, his mother stopped pestering him about marriage. But when a year had passed she sent a photograph of her candidate. Hari was disappointed, the girl had huge eyebrows, a double chin and bulbous cheeks sprinkled with acne. Hari calculated he could forestall the inevitable for another year and a half.

After two years Mrs Calloway was transferred to Jakarta and a new tenant moved in. His name was Bob Thompson and he worked for the World Bank. He was, Hari supposed, quite handsome, with thick blonde hair, pink and white skin and very pale blue eyes with long eyelashes. The staff under the Calloways had adjusted to a pleasantly dilatory routine: Hari hadn't bothered to clean behind the shelves and couches for over a year. But Bob wanted everything washed and polished and maintained at the highest level of cleanliness and order. He had the living room painted pale blue, the bedroom yellow, the bathrooms beige; he brought in a team of tailors to reupholster all the furniture; he bought curtains, rugs, paintings, lamps, deluxe air-conditioners, table cloths. He bought new uniforms for everyone, put Harmeet's son Balban on the staff and gave Hari lessons in mixing drinks and setting the table.

Bob had at least three dinner parties a week, a large cocktail party every fortnight and a dance party once a month. Harmeet boasted to Bob of having worked twice as hard at the German Embassy, but when Bob dismissed them on late nights, Harmeet moaned that keeping long hours hurt his eye and how his uncle had always warned him that the English were terrible masters. Hari was also daunted by the amount of work Bob's social life exacted; he'd grown accustomed to going to the cinema, sleeping late, playing cards in the garden at Khan Market. Now he was up at 6.30 and in bed at midnight.

But by far the most perplexing aspect of Bob's routine was that he saw several women in the course of a single week. Hari soon discerned three regulars. The first was Gerta, a stewardess from Lufthansa who always arrived at two in the morning in her flight uniform, pulling her portable luggage cart. The second was Joan, an English journalist who smoked and drank a lot and was always rude to the servants. Hari didn't think she was attractive at all—she wore round glasses and short skirts which exposed thin, unshaven legs. Hari fantasised about spilling oil on her dough-coloured thighs when he bent down to hand her the specially prepared gin and tonic she demanded. The third was Celeste, a French woman who'd come to Delhi fifteen years ago to study Bharatanatyam and teach ballet to the children of diplomats and businessmen. She wore nose-rings, peasant skirts hiked up over dance leotards and piles of silver jewellery like a Gujjar nomad, and always carried a huge bag with clothes, ankle bells, notebooks and incense. Of the three, Hari guessed that Celeste was the nicest because she wore Indian skirts.

The dhobi, who didn't speak any English, was severely taxed by the new demands on his time and skill, and had Hari translate when Bob called him in for laundry conferences. When Bob was out of town Hari went into the bedroom and tried on tuxedoes, shoes and silk shirts. He smelled Bob's cologne, tried his French cigarettes, used Bob's nail clipper and hairbrush. He then put on Bob's records and danced before the mirror, studying his reflection and his movements.

Hari considered stealing a shirt and tie. Bob had so many, he wouldn't notice. Hari could wear them when he went dancing at one of the hotels. One weekend, when Bob was in Madras for a nutrition conference, Hari took a shirt and tie back to his room and hid them in his trunk. He could hear Harmeet arguing with his wife; the servants rooms were very small. Hari thought in horror what Harmeet would say if he discovered the shirt or the tie. Harmeet's wife had keys to all the doors; sometimes she came into

Hari's room and started looking through his shelves when he was lying on the bed. Hari went numb with terror. He waited until Harmeet was drunk and his wife safely asleep, then crept into the house and put the shirt and tie back in Bob's closet. But once he was lying under his covers, he couldn't sleep, he still yearned to have the shirt, to see his friend's faces when he wore it.

Bob hired a second bearer named Surinder. He had flared nostrils from which thick hair protruded, a twisted mouth that did not close; his eyes were wedged so far into his skull, they were hardly visible. He slouched and shuffled, as if to make clear his distaste for work. Harmeet instantly commandeered Surinder's loyalty. Hari moved out of the way when the two older men settled on stools to discuss the belligerence and stupidity of foreign employers and to exchange black market information. Hari knew the servants from the German Embassy were selling quite openly from their employer's pantry. Harmeet defended buying German chocolate from them every week because there was no other way to get good chocolate in Delhi, and Bob had extremely high standards for desserts.

One morning Hari came into the kitchen and caught Harmeet doing something peculiar with a thermos and a bottle of vermouth. Harmeet immediately scolded Hari for not cleaning the floor. Hari wanted to shout back, but was afraid of Harmeet's temper and his seniority, so he grabbed his dusting towel and retreated into the dining room. Celeste sat at the breakfast table, reorganising her notebooks and using Bob's cellular telephone. She was onto her second cup of Bob's special Columbian coffee. She quickly learned where everything was hidden—the coffee, chocolates, liqueurs and soap. Hari often found her going through the cabinets, she was always perfectly nonchalant, she smiled and sometimes offered Hari a chocolate, which made him blush and shrink away.

"Hari, can you get me some more coffee?" She tapped the empty cup with her pencil. Hari reached for it and caught a whiff of her powerful smell, a mixture of patchouli perfume, perspiration, hair oil and charcoal—maybe it was the pencils she used, maybe she cooked on a charcoal stove. Hari went into the kitchen to heat some more coffee. Harmeet and Surinder sat in the driveway, slandering the servants down the block. When Hari returned to the living room, Celeste had pushed back the furniture and was doing her dance exercises in a purple leotard.

"Thanks, Hari," she smiled. Hari noticed her teeth were stained around the edges. It made Hari uneasy to look at her for too long, though he longed to study the contours of her underwear which were clearly visible beneath her leotard.

"Hey, Hari!" Ranjit cuffed Hari on the shoulder. Hari motioned towards Celeste, who was on the floor doing leg raises. Ranjit immediately straightened his posture.

"Good morning, Madame."

"Hello," Celeste smiled again, showing even more teeth. Ranjit discerned Celeste's accent and addressed her in French. Celeste moved to a chair, slid her legs onto the table and engaged Ranjit in what seemed a very pleasant, rather intimate discussion. Hari felt awkward holding his towel, waiting for them to switch back to English. Celeste shook out her multi-coloured hair and reached under her leotard to adjust the strap of her bra.

"Hey, Hari, has Bob got anymore of those Canadian cigarettes?"

"Yes, Ma'am." Hari went to the cabinet and opened a silver box and handed it to Celeste. Ranjit clicked a lighter the moment the cigarette touched her lips; they continued speaking in French. Hari pretended to dust the shelves, keeping a surreptitious eye on Ranjit. Ranjit no longer dressed like his other friends. His pants weren't flared at the bottom, he disdained bright colours and white shoes. At first Hari thought Ranjit looked dull, but after studying Bob he came to realise that Ranjit's new style was discreetly elegant. He was embarrassed at having spent so much money on a pair of white bell-bottoms. He resolved to sell them at Mohan Singh Market or send them to his mother.

After half an hour Celeste went into the bedroom to change. Ranjit and Hari shared a *bidi* in the driveway.

"She comes around a lot?" asked Ranjit.

"She's one of the regulars."

"He's got more?"

"One German, one English, lots of others for dinners and lunches."

"Not bad. Not bad at all," Ranjit nodded cannily. "You should study the guy. Find out all about his work. Look over his papers and books. That's how to get promoted. I started as a part-time, back-up driver; now I'm full time for the Consul General. The guy trusts me. I run all the secret errands to the embassy, secret files, picking up special guests at the airport." Ranjit winked. Hari was confused. Ranjit leaned forward and whispered, "And watch out for the other servants. They'll try to cut you out of the picture." Hari glanced anxiously at the chowkidar, who snored loudly at his post.

Celeste opened the kitchen door. Ranjit offered to give her a ride which she accepted. Hari watched Ranjit's car pull into the street, crushed his bidi against his heel and went back into the house.

Hari realised that he didn't know anything about Bob's work. He went into the study and opened Bob's shining bronze leather attache case. But he was nervous and almost spilled the cleaning liquid over it. It contained a silver pen, a manicure kit, two calculators and several reports from the World Bank. They were written in complicated English, with graphs and numbers about population density, triple-yield wheat and water purification. He gave up after five minutes, closed the attache case and went back to dust the living room.

But the morning had soured his mood. Everyone knew that the point of working for a foreigner was to procure a passage to the West. When Ranjit got a job as a back-up driver for the French Consul General, he bought French language tapes, teach-yourself books about accounting and an outline of French history. Hari realised that he ought to be more like Ranjit, to prepare and scheme. He had never approached life strategically, as something that required effort, risk and daring; he had always regarded it as something to enjoy, not to wage.

Nevertheless, Hari resolved to follow Ranjit's example and decided to put all his money into getting some new suits, shirts and ties. He considered how much he could keep for himself if he told his mother Bob had reduced his wages. With the extra he could buy some new clothes. It would take nine months to save enough to buy a good suit, like one of Bob's.

After dinner Hari wrote to his mother to say that his salary had been reduced and he would have to send less. But after he posted the letter in the morning he realised that it might provoke his mother to visit Delhi, a risk he could not afford to take. She would then produce the letters and plead with Bob for her poor daughters who needed husbands. He would have to send something to allay a crisis. There was an old silver tray left over from the Calloways' era. Hari reasoned that Bob wouldn't notice its absence. He could sell it, send the money to his mother, and say it was a bonus from his beneficent employer. The kitchen was Harmeet's territory, it would have to happen when a lot of people were around, during one of Bob's parties.

"Boy, I'm telling you . . ." Ranjit yawned, patted his thighs and stomach and lay across Hari's bed. "The boss, he is always away on some business. But his wife . . ."

"Good looking?"

"Not bad. Not bad at all. The other night I'm driving her back from a party in Hauz Khas. She has got on a new dress, new hair, the full thing. We drive into the house, I open the door for her. She asks me to come inside. She asks me to help her get out the brandy. Then she asks me to help her with the air-conditioner in the bedroom. So I go into the bedroom and I take care of the matter."

"And then?"

Ranjit yawned.

"Come on, tell!" Hari pelted Ranjit's shoulder.

"Well, then I have to help her relax and go to sleep." Ranjit sucked deeply on his cigarette.

"You weren't afraid?"

"Why afraid? It is part of my duty. Whatever they ask of us we have to provide. Such long hours . . ." Ranjit yawned again and squinted at a bathing suit ad in one of Hari's stolen magazines. Hari writhed his hands in his lap.

Hari first noticed Sara, an American, at one of the cocktail parties when she came into the kitchen and shook everyone's hand. She reappeared the following week at a dinner party. Again she came into the kitchen to praise the *palak paneer* and *nimbu* punch. Harmeet bowed and smiled. When she left he told Balban to stay away from her.

Hari thought Sara was pretty, even though she wore wilted skirts and peculiar rubber-soled loafers, and her hair was tangled at the back. She was very friendly, she always said Hello and asked the same questions foreigners always asked, Did he like Delhi? How many brothers and sisters? . . . and so on. Harmeet and Surinder agreed that she was probably from a low caste family back in America.

She had no regard for anyone's position or for manners—the way she just came into the kitchen and sat on the stool, helping herself to food and to other people's *bidis*. Gerta and Jane came in through the front door and sat in the living room and took food off trays when it was offered. Harmeet said the servants at the American Embassy always had stories of how crude and sloppy the tenants were.

Sara soon started spending nights. When Gerta, Joan or Celeste stayed over, Hari didn't think much about it, though sometimes he tried to see if anything was happening on the couch when he cleared the coffee and dessert dishes. But when Sara and Bob went into the bedroom and closed the door, Hari walked though the house on the pretense of clearing ashtrays or checking on lights so he could hover by the bedroom door to hear voices.

One night Hari heard the latest film hit playing in Bob's bedroom. He writhed in his bed, unbearably aroused. He crept into the house and ducked into the closet. He heard Sara and Bob laughing, furniture scraping the floor. The door opened, Sara came out, in her underwear. Hari crouched low so he could see through the slats in the door panels. Her skin was the same hue as her white underpants, her stomach sagged, her breasts hung limply under her raised arms. Sara went into the kitchen. Bob followed in a silk dressing gown; he would never wear underwear around the house. Hari heard glasses clinking against trays, the refrigerator door opening and closing, Sara giggling and Bob searching for the chocolate in the secret hiding place everyone knew about.

When they were back in the bedroom, Hari ran through the living room and the kitchen, through the garden and into his quarter. He threw himself on the bed and pulled the blanket over his head, his heart pounding, his ears assaulted by the collective snores of Harmeet's family.

Hari awoke early, went into the house and started dusting the china and crystal. Bob strode through the living room adjusting his tie and his cuff-links, glanced at the papers and took the car keys off the side table. Hari went back into the kitchen to polish the silver. Sara came in and sat down on the basket stool, rubbing her eyes.

"Hey, Hari, can I get some coffee with a lot of sugar?" Hari could not help staring at her nipples, pressed as they were against her translucent nightgown.

"Come sit and talk. Bob's gone to some conference, as always," she tugged on Hari's trousers. Hari nervously lowered himself onto the other basket stool, which belonged to Harmeet. Sara stirred her coffee with her index finger.

"Bob's a great guy. I bet he's a great boss."

"Yes."

"He works you guys pretty hard though."

"It's okay."

"He sees other women, doesn't he?"

"No." Hari felt moisture rise in his cheeks and palms.

"Come on, you can tell me. He does, doesn't he?" She raised her arms in a yawn, Hari tried desperately not to look. "Dammit Hari. I don't know what I'm doing here."

Sayeed, the new driver, opened the back door. Hari jumped up and pretended to wipe the basin. Sayeed squinted at Sara who was nonchalantly sipping her coffee, oblivious to the way the sun was now highlighting the contours of her thighs and stomach beneath her nightgown. Hari shoved some rupees into Sayeed's hand and told him to go to the market.

Hari again sat next to Sara. He had practised lowering himself into chairs in the living room when Bob was out of town, but now that he needed confidence, he felt clumsy. Sara rubbed her nose with the back of her hand. Hari couldn't tell if she was crying or if she had a cold.

"You know, Hari," she gulped her coffee and reached for a cookie on the counter, "I hate working at the embassy but I love being in India. I lived in Belgium before, you've no idea how boring it was. You're so lucky to be Indian. Don't you feel amazingly lucky?"

"I don't know." Hari didn't understand the question.

"If we embassy people didn't have servants we wouldn't learn anything about the countries we live in. Most of us never go anywhere but the embassy lounge, sometimes the Maurya coffee shop. The lady who sweeps my rooms is the only real Indian I know. I mean, I know Indians who wear suits but they don't count." Sara reached under her nightgown to scratch her stomach. The sheer fabric billowed above her legs, which were an even stranger colour in daylight. She was like a lost bird, if she'd only do something about her hair, Hari thought, and her fingernails.

"Hey, you know what I want to do? Go tomb-hunting."

"I'm sorry?"

"I want to go hunting through the old tombs around those posh South Delhi neighbourhoods. You don't have to work today, Bob's out till late. You can say you went with me."

Hari's heart pounded. He was anxious about what Bob might say. Mr Calloway never cared if Hari was in the house or not, the only person he needed was Harmeet. Sara reached for another cookie just as Harmeet and Sayeed came through the door. Hari bolted to his feet and started drying the already dry silverware. Harmeet sneered at Hari in guttural Punjabi, Hari glanced urgently at Sara.

"Hey, Harmeet, could I try one of those smokes of yours?"

Harmeet scowled. "What Memsahib?"

"Those *bidis,* can I have one?"

Harmeet froze. Sayeed took a *bidi* from his pocket, lit it on the stove and handed it to Sara. Sara inhaled deeply and coughed.

"Wow! I can't believe you smoke this stuff on a daily basis. I better get going. Hey Hari, tell Bob to call me."

Sayeed and Harmeet watched Sara amble towards the bedroom. Harmeet muttered disgustedly, Sayeed tried to get a last view of her torso through the nightgown.

A strange man started coming around whenever Bob wasn't at home. He always came through the back gate and asked for Surinder. Surinder would then take the man inside the house and through the garden. The man wore a peculiar turban. Harmeet was peculiarly reticent when Hari asked what the man was doing. He said the man was Surinder's astrologer and was helping him with an investment.

One evening Bob sat at the table, reading newspapers and absently chewing potato crisps. The compound was quiet, Harmeet had taken five days' leave to go to a wedding, Sayeed and Surinder smoked *bidis* in the driveway.

"Oh, Hari, some more butter if you would," Bob called as he took a roll without looking up.

"Yes, Sir." Hari put the butter dish on the table. "Sir?"

"Yes?" Bob glanced over the edge of his newspaper.

"May I ask you something?"

"What?"

"How come you aren't married?"

"Oh well, that's a real question." Bob put down the newspaper and pushed his chair away from the table. "I was almost married three times but it never worked out. You're not married yet yourself, isn't that right?"

Hari stared at his hands, "Not yet, but my mother has found a girl."

"Ah ha. Is she pretty?"

"No."

"Too bad, that'll make things difficult in the long run, I'd expect. Is she nice? That may matter a lot more."

"I haven't met her."

"You haven't? Odd custom you have with these arranged marriages, I can't see the value of doing it that way."

"Everyone does it."

"My friend Rumina wouldn't stand for it. Sit down, Hari." Bob pulled out a chair for him. This had never happened before, Bob was rarely alone at home, Harmeet was always hovering around. Hari sat. "Tell me Hari, do you want to get married?"

"I—I don't know."

"Have you got a choice?"

"I don't know." The notion of choice had never occurred to Hari before. Postponement yes, choice no. "Are you—do you want to get married, Mr Bob?"

"I don't need a family, I've got a lot of friends. I like having women around. And I like seeing different women, so if I got married, I'd be going into it knowing that I'd probably break the fidelity vow sooner rather than later. Of course, women see it all very differently. Women tend to fall in love quickly. I've fallen in love many times myself, that's not my problem, it's my dilemma. I'm always in love with several people at once. I say, Hari, you've been a great help."

"Me?"

"You've made life run so smoothly, handling my calls and all. You know, one never thinks about the people one sees every day as falling in love. I'm no good at guessing other people's feelings. How old are you?"

"Twenty-four."

"You should have some fun before you get dragged into marriage. Come, I want to give you something." Hari followed Bob into the bedroom. Bob took two suits out of the closet and lay them on the bed. "Try them on."

Hari had already tried them on a few weeks ago and they fit perfectly. He slipped one of the jackets over his shoulders and stared into the mirror as Bob adjusted the buttons and lapels

"Not bad, though the sleeves are a bit long. Take them.

They're not right on me these days. I don't know why, such lovely fabric. I had them made in Hong Kong."

"Thank you, Sir, thank you so much..."

"Quite alright. Just some old hand-me-downs."

Hari carried the suits back to his room and laid them on the bed, stunned and amazed. He could hardly sleep that night.

The next morning Hari was dusting picture frames when Bob came into the living room. Hari smiled and was about to speak when Bob's brusque request for coffee re-established Hari's conditioned timidity. Hari was wounded, but later assured himself that it was due to the presence of Surinder, who was slouched against the refrigerator, belching and muttering.

Hari's mother wrote with the news that she had arranged a date for Hari's wedding. Hari sunk into a foul mood. He felt very strongly that he did not want to marry someone he had not met. He was still afraid of his mother and would have to find a new method of postponing the marriage. He'd have to send some money and say that Bob had promised him another bonus if he did not take any time off for the following six months. He sent the letter the next morning.

After returning from the postbox, Hari went into the garden to pick some flowers for the evening's dinner party. He was about to step to the left of the patio, when, inexplicably, he turned and saw a huge cobra slide under the bushes, just where his left foot would have landed. Hari gasped—he had a huge fear of snakes from childhood. He ran back to the house and saw Surinder's astrologer slip through the back gate with two men in filthy dhotis. One of the men held a wicker basket which seemed to vibrate.

Hari remembered an incident from his childhood when one of his father's business associates had been fired and he had got a magician to put spells on Hari's family. His father had caught the man putting snakes and scorpions in the garden and had had him arrested for trespassing. For weeks afterwards everyone went to the temple and made elaborate offerings to the Goddess for the protection of the family. Hari's mother put amulets around the children's necks and gave everyone nicknames to ward off the evil eye.

Hari was sure that the men were magicians and Surinder was putting spells on either Bob or Harmeet or himself. Surinder never met his eyes when they passed in the hallway. He'd caught Surinder in Bob's bedroom, rifling through drawers. But he was afraid to say anything to Bob, lest Surinder found out.

That evening Bob asked Hari to help him get dressed for a dinner party. Bob studied his complexion and hair in the mirror. Hari was accustomed to seeing women sit before the mirror, toying with earrings, face cream, hair tonic, but never men. He wondered if he should mention the snake and the magician, but didn't know how to explain it.

The guests included Celeste, Jane, Bunky Singh, a Sikh journalist who Harmeet said was famous, and the new addition, Rumina. Hari stared at Rumina's highly conspicuous breasts as he bent over with a tray of *samosas* and peanuts. She had a grating voice, she gossiped viciously about who had money and who didn't, who was screwing whom (Ranjit told him what the word meant). She was extremely rude to the servants, which Harmeet and Sayeed expected, but Hari didn't like it, and thought of ways to avenge his pride. No one paid attention to Joan, who sulked in the corner, legs and arms crossed.

At the onset of dinner, Joan dominated the conversation with a boastful account of travelling through Iran and Iraq disguised as a man. Hari wasn't impressed, she looked like a man even when she wore a skirt. Hari pretended to reset the table so he could listen to the conversation. He couldn't follow everything; they were talking very fast and in strange accents. Bunky Singh started bellowing his point of view, Celeste ate peanuts and dangled one long purple leg over the other, Rumina's eyes kept turning towards a polite and remote Bob. Bob grinned and winked at Hari.

At 12.30 some of the guests started to leave. Hari emptied ashtrays, proffered brandy and brownies. He wanted to see how Bob was going to manage the three women. By 1.15 Joan, Rumina, Celeste, Bunky Singh, the Dutchman and Bob were faced off around the coffee table. Bunky Singh yawned, stretched one arm on the couch behind Celeste. Hari went into the kitchen to refill the ice bucket and the brownie tins. He heard a crescendo of voices, rushed towards the back door and saw Joan leaving with Bunky Singh and Celeste with the Dutchman. He crept through the kitchen and peered through the glass panel. Rumina was firmly rooted to the couch, Bob leaned over the stereo. Hari finished the dishes and was about to go to his room when he heard a car door slam. Celeste opened the kitchen door.

"Hi, Hari. Got any brandy?"

"Yes, Miss." He reached for the cabinet but she already had one hand on a bottle and another on a glass.

"See you." She paused long enough to wink, then headed towards the bedroom. Hari went outside and nudged the chowkidar who was drunk and nearly asleep. He asked if Rumina had left, the man muttered something affirmative. Hari went back into the kitchen to turn off the lights just as Bob came in, shirt unbuttoned, hair tousled.

"Oh, Hari, thanks so much for staying up so late."

"No mention, Sir."

"Before you turn in would you make sure all the doors and gates are locked?"

"No problem, Sir."

"Nightyo." Bob saluted and shut the door.

Hari bolted the front gate and checked the gate behind the servants' quarters. Harmeet's hadn't bothered to turn off his radio, which was churning static. Surinder's room was empty. Hari slipped back into the kitchen, took the old silver tray and hid it in his room. He went around the front to make sure the side garden door was closed. He crawled through the bushes to the space below Bob's bedroom window and pressed his ear against the wall. He heard muffled voices, an occasional thud, Celeste groaning strangely, another thud, Bob and Celeste laughing. Celeste started groaning again just as the next door chowkidar began his annoying hourly routine of whistling, stamping and pounding his stick. When the chowkidar finally stopped the bedroom was silent. Hari crawled back to his room, wiped the dirt off his knees and elbows and threw himself onto the bed.

He stared at the slivers of light that fell in filigree patterns on the frayed purple rug. He realised, for the first time, that he was profoundly dissatisfied. Nothing in his life had prepared him for these feelings and he didn't know what to do about them. Harmeet's family was perfectly content the way they lived; they didn't care about anything beyond food and films, they spat and coughed and left clothes and junk everywhere. Before Bob moved in Hari had never noticed, but now their habits disgusted him. He thought of his two years dusting the Calloways' shelves. His relationship with the Calloways consisted of a daily exchange of grunts and nods, requests given and services rendered. Mr Calloway asked for a cheese sandwich, Hari went into the kitchen and told Harmeet to make it. Hari then set it on the glass coffee table and Mr Calloway grunted, which meant either Thank You or I See You've Brought a Sandwich, Hari was never sure. That was it. Now he was engaged in Bob's life, but he wasn't sure whether he was a friend, a co-conspirator, a servant or a combination of all three.

He thought of his mother in Mussoorie, planning his wedding, of his older brother whose wife was expecting a third child. The Calloways had given him a week off to go to his brother's wedding. He'd enjoyed it so much at the time, but after seeing Bob's parties, he wondered if he'd enjoy it now. His mother expected him to send money for his sisters' dowries, and he had always sent it dutifully. That was what brothers did and he had never questioned it, but now he didn't want to take care of four older women. He wanted to spend his money on cigarettes, silk shirts, wine glasses, girlfriends. He'd gone to prostitutes but the rooms were filthy and the girls were sullen and bored and it was all over so quickly. Bob didn't go to dirty hotels in Old Delhi, Bob took women into his large, comfortable bedroom which Hari cleaned for him. Bob gave the girls wine and brandy and special brownies and cakes. Tears rose in Hari's eyes; he pounded his pillow, miserable and furious.

In the morning, Hari went to Khan Market and spent a full hour willfully loitering along the colonnade. No one was in when he returned, so he went to his room and ate three Swiss chocolates, which he'd taken off the dining room sideboard. Harmeet threw open Hari's door.

"Mr Bob has just sacked Surinder!"

"What?" Hari endeavoured to hide the French fashion magazine he was reading.

"When you were out in the market this morning, Mr Bob said he had caught him stealing and bringing strangers into the house. He gave him one month's pay and told him to get out at once. Surinder yelled back at Mr Bob; he said that Mr Bob was a liar, that we were the ones who were stealing. My goodness, God!" Harmeet moaned and clutched his hands to his heart. "Mr Bob, Sayeed and I went into Surinder's room and watched him pack his trunk. Mr Bob gave him a train ticket to Bhopal and had Sayeed drive him to Old Delhi station!" Hari hardly listened, he could only think of the silver tray in his trunk.

Bob summoned Hari and Harmeet into the living room. He wore a new turquoise silk dressing gown which matched his turquoise eyes, his left knee bobbed up and down over the right, a newspaper was open on his lap.

"Sit down, fellows."

Hari and Harmeet lowered themselves onto the edge of the couch.

"I've dismissed Surinder. I gave him one month's severance pay and a train ticket to Bhopal. I have clear proof that he was stealing. On several occasions I found him prowling about the kitchen and godown at night. Yesterday I caught him in my bedroom, I asked him to leave the room and my gold cuff-links fell out of his pocket. I believe he was part of a racket of thieves. I'm not sorry he's gone, he was a sloppy fellow and he wasn't very pleasant to have around. You two needn't worry about your jobs. I sensed that neither of you were particularly loyal to Surinder and we'll all be much happier now that he's gone. I don't like stealing. I understand the pressure that you're under, supporting relatives and all, but I'd prefer it if you spoke with me directly if you need or want something. Do we understand each other?"

They nodded in unison.

"So the matter is closed." Bob picked up his newspaper. Hari and Harmeet shuffled out.

Bob assembled the staff to plan his next dance party. Bob had lived in Rio de Janiero prior to India. He had the tailor make special Brazilian costumes for the staff, he hired ten extra bearers to help with the food and drinks and a band from Goa called Tinky and His Tornadoes, and he sent out over five hundred invitations.

Celeste, Gerta, Jane, Sara and Rumina were among the first to arrive. Gerta looked different out of uniform—she wore tight blue pants and a ruffled blouse. Celeste's hair was coiled on top of her head, she wore heavy make-up, a nosering, anklets, black leotards and a purple *lungi.*

Hari wondered if they knew about each other. He watched with amazement as Bob maneuvered his way through the party, negotiating the women with a quick dance here, a bedroom conference there, a surreptitious squeeze on a hip, a kiss on an ear. Harmeet, Sayeed and Balban gaped at the Indian girls in short skirts. Celeste danced mildly in a corner with Bunky Singh.

By 10.30 Sara was drunk. Her cheeks were flushed bright red, she howled snatches of lyrics. People were looking at her; her dress had slipped off her left shoulder, showing a large portion of her brassiere. Hari scanned the room for Bob. He went down the hall to the back bedroom and came upon Bob and Joan huddled on the bed. Hari quickly shut the door and headed down the hall. As he turned the corner Bob tapped his shoulder.

"Thanks for the help, old man. We'll have to keep the girls apart. Do me a favor and go dance with Sara, I think she's had a bit too much punch." Bob nudged Hari towards the dance-floor where Sara had her arms and legs around her hapless partner. Hari cautiously touched Sara's arm, she seized his hands and did a vigorous twist. He attempted to follow what she was doing. Though nervous at first he soon mastered the movements and started adding a few ideas of his own. He noticed some girls watching him, he hoped he looked good in the shirt made by Bob's tailor. He considered having a glass of punch, but caught Harmeet's glare and decided to wait.

The party went on till 4.30 in the morning. Sara threw up in the garden and had to be carried to the taxi. Celeste left with Bunky Singh. Joan got into an argument with one of Bob's World Bank colleagues. Rumina disappeared early. Before he went to bed Hari noticed Gerta's luggage cart tucked behind Bob's dresser. At 5.30, as soon as Hari heard Harmeet's snores, he took the silver tray out of his trunk and put it back in the kitchen. When he closed his door, he nearly fainted with relief.

The following weekend Bob was out of town. Hari sat alone in the living room, watching the BBC news on Bob's TV. He heard the front bell, it was Sara. She looked very pretty, much prettier than usual; she wore a pink silk dress with matching shoes and she'd managed to comb all her hair into one line.

"Hi, Hari. Tell Bob we're late."

"Mr Bob has just gone to Bombay."

"But I've got tickets to a show."

"Come inside." Hari led Sara into the living room. He started to pour a soda for her when she pulled him to the couch.

"Did he go with that English writer woman?"

"No, no, he has just gone for a conference."

"He went with her, I'm sure." She shuddered and pressed her face into her arm. "It's my fault. I behaved so stupidly at the party. He's mad at me, I know it. I don't even remember what happened. I just had three rum punches and then everything was spinning around. Was everyone talking about me after I left?"

"No, no, nobody said anything at all." Hari tried to sound resolute.

Sara slouched into the pillows, her fist pushed against her mouth, then grabbed Hari's arm. "Come with me. I've got these tickets to the show at Pragati Maidan and I'm not going to waste them. Go put on a jacket, and hurry!"

Hari ran into his room, put on the jacket Bob had given him, nervously combed his hair, adjusted his belt and trousers. The television was blaring in Harmeet's room. Hari ran out of the gate and got into the taxi next to Sara. He was excited, he only went to shows if they were free, like the government-sponsored *melas* that happened in the winter.

The first item was a circus troupe from Taiwan. Hari enjoyed it immensely, especially the clown character. The second item was an Australian ballet, Sara liked it a lot more than he did. The ballet was followed by a Polish jazz quartet and a Belgian avant-garde theatre piece with people in black costumes and white and orange face paint doing what looked like karate. At intermission Sara turned and waved to a group of Americans sitting a few rows behind.

"Hi guys! Hari, this is Jill, Susan, Bruce and Gary." Gary and Bruce glared at Hari with overt suspicion. Gary was the more alarming of the two, his skin, hair and eyes were all of the same flat hue of beige, his arms were almost the size of Hari's legs.

"This show's kinda spent. Wanna go dancing?"

"Sure!" Hari trailed behind as they piled into a white embassy van and drove to the Taj Hotel. The Americans chattered loudly about the embassy. Hari endeavoured to appear nonchalant as he glanced out of the window with his hands in his pockets. They arrived at the Taj Hotel and went downstairs to the disco. The Polo Club had booked it for a private party, so they went back upstairs to the all-night coffee shop.

Hari had fantasised vividly about having a late night meal in such a coffee shop, wearing one of Bob's suits and possibly talking to a girl. Now he was wearing Bob's suit and presumably talking to Sara, but he was also crammed next to Bruce which made him very nervous. Gary asked the waiter for a double cheese burger with fries, the waiter said they didn't serve cheese burgers. Gary pounded his fist on the table and demanded to see the manager. Hari watched the scene with anguish, afraid the hulking beige man would turn the wrath he so clearly felt towards the Indian subcontinent on its most proximate representative, which, in the waiter's absence, was himself.

"You know what, if the Indians just cut out this sacred cow thing and started eating meat, they wouldn't have a starvation problem."

"You're wrong, it takes ten times more land and grain to make a pound of beef protein that a pound of milk," replied Sara vehemently.

"Oh yeah? Since when are you Miss Nutrition Expert?"

"I'm stating a well-known fact."

"I'm sorry, Sir, what is the problem?" The manager, in a blue silk jacket and tie, leaned solicitously towards Gary.

"I want a goddamn cheese burger, for Chrissakes, is that asking for too much?"

"I'm afraid we don't serve cheese burgers. May I bring you something else?"

Gary tossed his glass of water across the floor. Sara hoisted Gary to his feet. "I do apologise for my colleague's behaviour."

"No mention, Madame." The manager bowed graciously to Sara and shot Hari a peculiar look. Sara led the group outside, pushed Hari into a taxi and sat beside him.

"Where're you goin'?" snarled Gary.

"You acted like a real creep, Gary. It was embarrassing."

"Hey, who's that guy you're with?" Gary thrust a pulpy finger towards Hari.

"He's a friend of mine."

"The protocol people aren't gonna like it!" Gary shouted as the taxi pulled into the street.

"Does that man work at the embassy?" asked Hari when they were safely on the road.

"No, he's just a high school kid. I have to pretend to be nice to him because his dad is one of my bosses at the USIS. I guess we should forgive him for his stupidity." Sara thrust her head out of the window. "I love the way India smells. It's this amazing combination of smoke and dirt and flowers. America smells of gasoline and hot dogs."

They pulled into Malcha Marg, paid the taxi and walked upstairs to Sara's second-storey flat. There were clothes and shoes strewn on the floor and couches, dust balls and spider webs dangled in the corners. A batik wall-hanging of

Shiva blowing a conch hung from a crooked bamboo rod, the mirror was pasted over with postcards. Every table and chair was loaded with fans, bowls, basket stools and umbrellas, all of which had no apparent relation to anything else.

"I know it's a big mess, I'm really bad at cleaning up stuff."

"You haven't got a bearer?"

"My landlord sends up a sweeper lady once a week and a cook sometimes. Come in here, there's more space in the bedroom." Hari peered timorously through the doorway. The bed was covered with silk pillows, magazines and half-eaten chocolate bars. Sara pushed some of the pillows and magazines onto the floor so Hari could sit down.

"Have you heard this? My latest obsession." The tape player let loose the violin strains of the latest Hindi film hit.

"You really like this music?"

"I think it's the most wildly romantic, bizarre, fantastic pop confection I've ever heard!" Sara moaned and fell backwards onto the pillows. Hari considered that maybe she wasn't faking it. Suddenly she clutched her heart and looked desperately sad. "Oh Hari, help me, I don't know what I'm doing here."

"You don't like this flat?"

"No, here in Delhi. I hate working at that stupid American Library. My friend Clara has a great job, she works for the Ford Foundation on women's development. She gets to live in villages, she travels all over. I just shelve books in Connaught Place." Sara clutched a pillow and rolled onto her side, facing Hari, who slid his legs onto the bed and knocked over several magazines and two chocolate bars.

"Just leave it, I don't care. Hari, do you want to travel?"

"Yes, we all want to travel."

"Who's we?"

"It's hard for Indians to get passports."

"Do you have a passport?"

"I got one through my uncle but I've never used it."

"But why would you want to leave India?"

"Everyone in my family tells me I can have a better life in the West."

"Oh, wait, this is the best part!" Sara turned up the volume, closed her eyes and swayed her hands in the air. Hari wondered if he'd said the right thing about wanting to travel. He didn't want Sara to think he liked her because she worked at a foreign embassy. The song rose to a climax, then faded away. Sara turned her face into the mattress and sobbed.

"I'm so unhappy. I shouldn't be in love with Bob, I know he's got five other girl friends. It always happens to me like this. I can't ever get the people I love to fall in love with me." Hari put his hand on her shoulder and leaned down to kiss her forehead. She seized his arms and kissed him frantically on his face and neck. "Don't stop, don't . . ." The moment she spoke he wondered if indeed he should stop, but she kept clutching his arms and shoulders and moving her mouth over his face. He shut his eyes and lunged at her. She unbuttoned his shirt, he pulled up her dress and pressed his hips into hers. She moaned and ran her hands over his back and legs.

Hari had anticipated something quite different, something similar to what he had seen in movies, when the girl, ever timid, was either gently wooed or brutally conquered. Prostitutes just lay down and stared at the ceiling and waited for him to finish. He never imagined a girl with a good job behaving this way. Sara pulled off her dress and lay on top of him. Hari was shocked. He held his breath, afraid of what she might do next. Suddenly she yelled and collapsed, panting on the bed. Hari exhaled.

"Oh, Hari . . ." Sara put her arms around him and lay her head against his stomach. He stroked her hair, which was amazingly soft, like a kitten's fur. Soon she was asleep, and he felt safe enough to fall asleep too.

When Hari awoke, the clock read 10.30. Sara was in the shower, singing a film song with a peculiar sequence of Hindi syllables. Hari sat up and pulled the bedsheet to his waist. He lit one of the English cigarettes on the side table, tried and failed to blow a smoke ring like the way he'd seen it done in a film Ranjit took him to see at the French Cultural Centre.

The dressing table was overloaded with half-filled bottles of lotion, hair-spray and nail polish. Clothes lay in crumpled piles, underwears, socks, brassieres. Harmeet's family never bothered to fold their clothes or make their bed, but Harmeet was a cook and Sara was an American. She was so bewilderingly different from Bob, who was incapable of making a mess. Bob instinctively folded newspapers when he finished reading them, he swept what breakfast crumbs had fallen off the plate into his hand and deposited them in the wastebasket, he was irritable if he found his shoes, jackets and ties out of their proper sequence in the closet.

Sara came out of the bathroom, wrapped in a pink towel. "Let's go out for breakfast. You don't have to work, do you? It's Sunday."

"No . . ." He tried to get a hold of her hand but she went back into the bathroom. He pulled on his trousers and shirt, flattened his hair with his palms, smoothed out the wrinkles in his beautiful silk jacket. Sara emerged in a blue dress and a Kashmiri shawl. They walked to the cab-stand and drove to a sweet shop in Sunder Nagar Market.

"My friend Clara brought me here. It has those great South Indian rolled things."

"Dosas?"

"Is that what they're called? I like those pizzaesque things too, with coconut sauce." They ordered *dosas*, *idlis* and *uttapams*. Birds clustered around small puddles left by the night rain, the air carried scents from flowering trees. Sara had her feet up on the opposite chair and ate with her hands, as he did. Hari felt a surge of pride and wonder. Not only had he spent the night with Sara but now he was having breakfast with her. He had a genuine secret life now, it no longer consisted of sneaking into Bob's room to try on clothes. He wondered how he should describe it to Ranjit.

After breakfast Sara and Hari went tomb-hunting. They went first to Humayan's tomb, then to Moth-ki-Masjid and Masjid-ki-Moth, Hauz Khas, the Qutb complex and Jamali-Kamali. At dusk they sat in Lodi Gardens and watched the sky fill with orange light. The drone of birds and insects swelled as the sky darkened. A *baul* singer wandered through the old tombs, singing praises to Krishna. When the uppermost clouds turned from red to purple they walked to the cab-stand. Sara kissed Hari goodbye and went home.

Hari took a long time on his way back to Bob's. He paused to smell clusters of jasmine, to chat with the *bhelpuriwalla,* to welcome the evening star which scintillated over the minarets of Safdarjang's tomb. When he opened Bob's gate and headed towards his room he heard a disturbingly familiar voice in the living room. He peered into the main house and saw his mother sitting with Bob.

"Ah, Hari, we were wondering where you were," Bob shook Hari's hand forcefully. Hari was too stunned to notice whether Bob was irritated or not. It was Sunday, technically his day off, and Bob was supposed to be in Bombay, or was there a last-minute dinner plan and was he in disgrace? He made a clumsy *namaste* to his mother and sat on the edge of a chair.

"I know I have taken the household by surprise," said Mrs Rajan. "But once in a while a mother has got to see her son in person. A photo will not suffice." She gazed at Hari with maternal beneficence and winked back at Bob. Hari speculated in horror about what information had possibly been divulged over tea.

"You've never considered moving to Delhi, Mrs Rajan?" asked Bob.

"After Hari's father passed away, shifting from Mussorrie became an impossibility. One has got so many friends and acquaintances already there." Mrs Rajan took another of Harmeet's sugar cookies and smiled. "How nicely the cook has done it."

"If you'll excuse me I've got an urgent appointment which called me back from Bombay. It was lovely meeting you, Mrs Rajan, I hope I shall see you again before you go." Bob bowed to Hari's mother and went out of the front door.

"What a lovely person! Such manners he has got. And so good looking." Mrs Rajan peered at the drapes, pillows, brass bowls and *bidri* boxes about the room. "So much to keep tidy. I can see you must be working very hard."

"So hard you cannot imagine," Hari hung his head in an effort to appear weary and dutiful.

"But how can such a rich man reduce wages with a clear conscience? These Englishmen are not concerned with the plight of a poor Indian family."

"He is my master, I must do what is required."

Mrs Rajan clucked and shook her head. "Perhaps he can do something for your sister Pritti."

"I'll make an inquiry." Hari saw Harmeet's face against the glass panel in the door and swiftly steered his mother out of the house and into his little room in the back. Mrs Rajan sat on the bed and took a full perusal of the stack of European magazines, the frayed rug, the new suit hanging on the wall. Hari winced.

"From where did you get this suit?"

"Mr Bob lets me use it when we have special parties."

"My goodness," she smiled proudly. "So Hari, the date has been set."

"What date?"

"The date of your wedding. We have booked the rooms at the hotel and have even advanced money to the caterer. We are hoping you will come soon to meet with the family. I have already asked Mr Bob for some leave for you."

"Mother, you shouldn't have done that."

"Why not? He was very happy to grant."

"But there are others who . . ." he knelt by the bed and whispered, "The cook's family does not want to see me advance. Balban, the son, is trying to supplant me here. I have to be in the house at all times!"

"So why were you out since this morning? All day I have been waiting."

"Today was the first holiday I have had in months. You mustn't interfere, Ranjit is advising me."

"Oh . . ." Her eyes widened as she drew her fingers protectively to the gold chain which nestled in the folds of her neck. "Ranjit has done very well for himself. His mother tells me they are considering him for a foreign posting."

Hari was relieved that the mention of Ranjit, his father's brother's eldest son and a perpetual family favourite, had for the moment reversed things in his favour. He heard Harmeet's wife berating her daughter-in-law. He knew he couldn't get rid of his mother till the morning, but he had to keep her as far from Harmeet's family as possible.

"Mother, I want to take you out to dinner."

"But what of keeping your posting?"

"Sunday night I can go out. Mr Bob is not in for dinner." He led her into the street, hailed a scooter and directed it to the South Extension Market where he'd seen a tandoori restaurant. It cost a lot of money but he had no choice, he had to keep his mother pacified and subjugated. Mrs Rajan was very impressed with the decor and the food, though she clucked disapprovingly at the way the Delhi women cut their hair so short. After dinner they strolled through the arcade. Mrs Rajan paused in front of the shop windows to study sari borders, hosiery, earrings and suitings.

By 7.30 the next morning, Mrs Rajan was in the courtyard with Harmeet's wife. Hari knew a comparative study of weddings was inevitable. He encouraged his mother to go shopping in the afternoon, which she did, with Harmeet's daughter-in-law. Hari couldn't concentrate on anything and twice emptied the wastebaskets into the laundry baskets. It was clear that his mother intended to stay until he was given leave to return to Mussoorie with her.

In the evening Harmeet's family burst into Hari's room with sweets and garlands to celebrate his impending marriage.

"Mr Bob?"

"Oh, Hari, I was about to call you. I need some help with these shoes. They got horribly scuffed up in Bombay." Hari took the shoes and searched for the polish and brush. One of the shoes dropped from Hari's quaking hand.

"What's the matter, old man, have you got that head cold of Harmeet's?"

"No, I—I must ask for your help."

"Oh, I see—what is it?" Bob instantly became cordial and motioned Hari to sit beside him on the bed.

"My mother wants me to go to Mussorrie in two weeks to meet with the girl's family. She has already advanced money to the caterer. I can't postpone it any longer."

"Oh my. Now tell me again why don't you want to marry this girl."

"I don't want to marry someone I've never met."

"That seems perfectly reasonable. I don't consider marriage until the affair's been going for two years minimum. So how do you get out of it?"

"I don't know. Now that my mother's met you, she won't believe me if I tell her that you won't give me leave."

"Gosh, I am sorry about that, Hari. So let's think hard for a minute here." Bob tapped his fist against his sharp pink chin. What if you tell her you've found someone of your own preference?"

Hari thought about this for a moment. His psyche was equipped to perform small gestures of prevarication, but Bob's suggestion was an act of extraordinary defiance. His mother would insist on meeting the girls' family, and the only girl he had met in Delhi that he liked was Sara, who was so absolutely out of the question.

"Mr Bob, maybe if you ask my mother she will accept another postponement."

"But it seems to me that you don't want to postpone the thing, you want to get out of it altogether, correct?"

"Yes." Hari flushed with shame.

"Let me have a good long think about this. I've got to get dressed, Celeste will be here any minute. If Rumina or Sara calls, tell them I'm at a conference at one of the hotels. Don't say which hotel, Rumina will have her spies after me. And do what you can with that shoe." Bob went into the shower. Hari knelt to buff the shoe. He was suddenly repulsed at the idea of lying to Bob's girlfriends. He'd enjoyed it before, it gave him a jolt of excitement whenever he kept one of the women at bay, steered her off course. He was an indispensable part of Bob's intricate balancing act, a comrade in masculine arms. But now it shamed him, and he had to admit it, he was jealous that Sara preferred Bob's company to his.

"Hari, what is the matter?"

"Nothing, Ma . . ."

The door swung open, it was Sara, smiling eagerly.

"Hari! Why haven't you come to see me?"

"Who is it?" Mrs Rajan pushed through the door before Hari could stop her.

"Sara, this is my mother."

"Oh, hi! I didn't know Hari had a mother!"

"But all boys have a mother," said Mrs Rajan.

"I know, I know, but you know what I mean, a real, living mother that I could—like—meet at his house."

Hari stood dumbly in the doorway. It was one thing for Bob to meet his mother, it was quite another for Sara to meet her. His mind was so numbed with terror that he watched but did not register what was happening—that Sara and Mrs Rajan were making tea and sitting down on the *bersati* to drink it.

"Come on, Hari, sit with us," Sara patted the seat next to her. Hari obeyed, wondering what to do should Sara drop a suggestion of what had happened between them.

"When Hari was a young boy he was always taking things from the kitchen!" Mrs Ranjan chuckled and dipped her sugar cookie neatly into her tea.

"Where did Hari grow up?"

"In Mussorrie. Such a lovely place. Come and stay with us."

"I'd love to! In two months Delhi will be a sweat box and a half and we'll have to flee for our lives." Sara pulled her knees to her chest which caused her skirt to slip up her thighs. Hari observed his mother's shock, fresh waves of perspiration burst through his skin.

"Why don't you come for Hari's wedding?"

"Hari's wedding?"

"So much effort we have already made. And such a nice girl. One can rest at night only when one knows that one's son is being well looked after."

Sara turned to Hari, "You never told me about this."

"It's not settled..."

"Yes, it is fully settled." Mrs Rajan smoothed her flowered rayon sari over her knees.

"Mother..." Hari ran into the kitchen, down the drive and out of the gate.

"Hari!" Sara ran after him. "Hey, stop it!" She pulled his arm, they both fell down. "You're getting married and you never told me?"

"It's not, it's—I've never even met the girl!" Hari burned at the humiliation of trying to explain something Sara wouldn't understand.

"You've never even met ? Not even for dinner?"

"This is the way it's done."

A car careened round the corner. Hari grabbed hold of Sara before she fell into the nullah, then pulled away in embarrassment.

"We have to go talk somewhere. Where do you want to go?"

"I don't care."

"Think of something!"

"You think of something!"

Sara flagged a scooter and told the driver to go to the Taj Hotel. Hari watched the trucks, the road, the Shiva lingams, the pariah dogs, the Muslim graves. He wanted to cry. They stopped outside the hotel and walked through the bushes to the pool. Hari stared morosely at the pool.

Sara seized his hand, "Now I get it. It's an arranged marriage."

Hari nodded. Sara gazed bemusedly into the turquoise water, broken by the gyrations of a single swimmer. "Can't you just say No Thanks, I'd rather figure this out on my own?" Hari shook his head. "Why not?" Hari glared. "Sorry. So what are you going to do?" Hari pressed his palm against his forehead. "I was waiting for you to call me."

Sara pulled his hand to her heart and rested her head on his shoulder. Hari frowned, was he supposed to call her? The moon shone from behind a gauze of blue clouds. The swimmer lay still in the middle of the pool.

"I don't understand this country. It's the most romantic place I've ever been to but everyone has an arranged marriage. Maybe that's why it's so romantic, no one gets to fall in love so they spend their whole lives dreaming about it. In America we start having affairs when we're fourteen. By the time we're twenty-one we're cynics. Everyone's had so much sex and read so many articles and books about sex it's not romantic or mysterious, it's something you do in addition to having dinner."

Hari tried to make sense of what she was saying. The swimmer pulled himself up the ladder and walked towards the hotel. A swarm of thoughts and feelings collided in Hari's brain. He wanted to suspend time and action to stay frozen in the moon-soaked garden, inhaling jasmine, feeling Sara's head on his shoulder. At twelve o'clock, they walked home. When Hari was sure that his mother was asleep, they sat on the *bersati*. Their fingers entwined, Sara kissed Hari's neck, Hari touched her leg. Suddenly Bob slid open the screen door.

"Goodness, Sara, oh, it's Hari with you! Aren't you getting attacked by mosquitoes?"

"No, it's beautiful out here. Can I have a coke?"

"Surely. Hari, would you?"

"Yes, Sir." Hari bolted into the kitchen. His hands trembled so fiercely that he could hardly turn the ice tray. He heard the pantry door click, he swerved round, and saw Celeste opening a jar of chocolate almonds.

"Hi, Hari." She leaned against the counter and chewed. Hari accidently pulled out the silver tray that he had almost sent to his mother, shrieked and dropped it on the floor.

"Are you okay?" Sara put her head through the door. "Oh, Celeste, hi!"

"Hi." Celeste waved three fingers and continued chewing almonds.

"Come sit on the porch." Sara took the coke from Hari's hand. Celeste sauntered out after Sara.

Bob peered through the door. "Hari, fix me a gin and tonic, would you? Then go ahead and turn in for the night."

"Yes, Sir." Hari made the drink and carried it to the *bersati*. No one looked at him. Sara's voice rose excitedly above Bob and Celeste's laughter. He went into his room and unrolled his bedding on the floor. Mrs Rajan snored loudly, her blankets were on the floor, her hands splayed over her round stomach.

Hari writhed furiously. It was suffocating, his mother's snores, Sara's trills of laughter, Bob's commands, Harmeet's radio. He laced and unlaced his fingers. It was 2.30, the night withheld sleep, oblivion or resolution. He took his blanket and went into the courtyard. The moon cast everything in silver, the air smelled of fresh grass. He sat in the corner, wondering what to do. By morning he decided to sell the suits Bob had given him and leave Delhi.

At nine the next morning, Hari took one of the suits to Mohan Singh Place and sold it. He winced to part with it, even though the salesman gave him a good price. He decided to keep the second suit in case he needed money later. He spent the rest of the day wandering through Connaught Place. He had a large lunch at Regal Coffee House, bought a map of India, a train schedule and a spy novel. He sat by the central fountain and planned his journey. First Bhopal, to stay with his cousin Amar, then to Bombay where he could find a job as a waiter. He never wanted to see Bob or Sara again. They had wounded him, though he didn't know precisely why. They had raised an expectation of friendship and had cruelly dashed it. They pretended to care about him, but in the end he was only a servant.

Hari knew Bob was going to a cocktail party at six. At 6.30 p.m. he went back to the house to pack his things. He slipped through the back gate and headed for his room when Bob opened the kitchen door.

"Hari, come in here. I've been waiting for you all day." Hari wondered whether to run, but an instinct for obedience made him follow Bob into the bedroom. Bob shut the door and motioned to Hari to sit on the bed. "I think I've got a solution for you. I'm being transferred back to the World Bank headquarters in Washington. I've decided to take you with me. I'm afraid I've been spoiled by all my years in the Third World. I just don't want to spend the time looking after my clothes and preparing my own dinner. I'll arrange your travel documents and visas through the bank. I doubt that your mother will stand in the way of your going abroad. I do hope your fiancée will be able to find another candidate."

"You're going to Washington?"

"Yes, and so are you, rather sooner than I'd expected, which is quite alright, given the awful weather that's coming up. We're going in three weeks."

"Three weeks?"

"Yes. I'll need your help getting everything packed up. Don't look so worried, I suspect you'll rather like it over there. By the way, this was Sara's idea. You were very sweet to look after her last night, thanks a million. She'll be coming with us, she's decided to move back to the States as well."

Harmeet and Balban were alarmed that Hari was going to America and tried to schedule a private conference with Bob to persuade him to reconsider, but Bob had meetings in Calcutta and Hyderabad. Mrs Rajan passed the days alternately weeping and rejoicing. Ranjit came over every evening to reassure her of Hari's tremendous good fortune. It became the sole topic of discussion in every servant's quarter in the neighbourhood.

Hari supervised all the packing, especially of Bob's wardrobe. Bob rewarded him with three new suits. Ranjit hosted a farewell party at the Tandoor House in South Extension. Bob gave Mrs Rajan a huge sum of money which covered all the expenses of her daughter's dowries and obliterated all concerns about Hari's wedding plans.

The day arrived. All the bags were packed, the house was empty. Hari stood in the gateway, wearing one of Bob's suits with a new pair of shoes. He watched the *bhelpuriwalla* pack his box and heave it onto his shoulder. Soon the car would come to take him to the airport and he would leave the garden, the banyan trees, the parrots, the old women resting on *charpois* across the road. He realised that he had no idea where he was going and how he would live. He would be able to take girls out to dinner and bring them back to his house without Harmeet watching over him. He would be able to buy more shoes and shirts and ties and radios. But now all that mattered was the scent of *puris,* charcoal and *mogra* in the evening air, the sound of temple bells, bicycle chimes and bird calls, the old cow wandering towards him in the dark street. He had never been without these things and he never realised that he loved them. Tears streamed down his face. He dropped his bags on the ground and wondered if he should tell his mother that he would marry the girl, or whether he should just go back to his room and hide.

But it was too late, the World Bank jeep was already turning into the drive, and Sara and Bob were waving from the back seat. Hari dried his face on his sleeve, picked up his bags and ambled towards the jeep. Sayeed and Harmeet's families came out to cover him in garlands. He pressed the soft marigolds to his cheeks and allowed himself a few more tears.

The Visa

KITTEN PUSHED MELANIE FORWARD. "ZEENIE, you know Melanie, Beenu's old school mate. See, I've already given her a *deshi* look." Zeenat traced two fingers over Melanie's orange silk *salwar kameez,* took her hand and led her towards the crowd of politicians, diplomats, film stars, journalists and astrologers that murmured and drank and smoked about the lawn. "Sanjeev, Bina, Lalu, this is Melanie Andrews. She works at the US Embassy, so we must show her a good time. Lalu is an interior designer, Sanjeev works with *The Hindustan Times,* so you can use him as a source whenever you like."

Lalu surveyed Melanie's costume. "I see you have developed a fondness for our Indian dress."

"The embroidery is just so beautiful!" Melanie patted the tiny gold threads woven through the silk. Lalu counted three broken fingernails on Melanie's hands.

"Our garments are most suitable for our weather," said Mr Tandon.

"Have you considered a sari, Miss Andrews?" Bina took scrupulous inventory of Melanie's bony torso, softened a little by the loose orange silk, and of her dull hair and skin, two planes of beige broken by faint blue eyes.

"Do you think it would go on me? I'm so—so American-looking."

"Not to worry, our sari can be draped in a multitude of styles, yet it is but a single rectangle of cloth."

"Melanie, I've got someone for you to meet." Kitten pushed forward a slender young man wrapped in a white shawl. "Hari, say hello, don't be so rude."

"Hello, Miss Andrews." Hari brushed a thick strand of hair off his cheek and glanced at Melanie with a beatific smile.

"Melanie, have a kebab." Zeenat held out a plate of kebab sticks. "So, is your embassy job enticing?"

"Well, yes, but India is much more enticing!" The crowd chuckled politely. Cool streams of air brushed Melanie's forehead. She remembered how disappointed she was when she first learned that the State Department had transferred her to India. She had come prepared for heat, crowds and frustration, but instead she found sublime gardens, bungalows and marvellous friends. Her last post was Tunis where few people spoke English and what meagre social life there was found its only nourishment at the American Club movie theatre. In Delhi, there were parties and concerts and exhibitions every night, everyone spoke exquisite English and dressed so beautifully and belonged to enormous complicated families.

"So much for politics, we've got some *filmwalas* here tonight. Goodness, you're without a beverage." Zeenat raised a jewelled hand to summon a bearer, then paused midair to signal three men wearing cricket caps and white *kurtas.*

"Bikram, how can you bring your cricket ruffians to a respectable party? Give a kiss." Zeenat's fingers slid down Bikram's arm to clasp his hand. "Come, meet a very nice American lady and please behave nicely when you do."

Bikram squeezed Melanie's hand. "How is it that we've not met before?"

"Let that woman go! I'm sorry, I didn't get your name."

"Melanie."

"I'm Kiran. Those two are Arun and Vinod."

Vinod kissed Melanie's hand. "They make them so prettily over there."

"Oh buck off, Vinod. Don't listen to him, Miss Andrews . . ."

Drumbeats sounded from the rose bushes, a team of acrobats and jugglers rushed onto the lawn. Melanie watched delightedly, children screamed and laughed, spangled costumes streaked the air.

"Why Zeenat insists on having these scruffy acrobats invade our fun, God knows." Vinod peered at Melanie over the rim of his scotch glass.

"You don't think they're wonderful?"

"This is fine for villagers but it puts me to sleep. Why don't we check out of here and go dancing?"

"I've come with—"

"Kitten? Bring her along. Kiran, round up the crew and let's pack off." Vinod steered Melanie towards the driveway.

"Shouldn't we say goodbye to the Shahs?"

"Only if you want to stay five more hours." Melanie gazed back at the acrobats as the car pulled away.

Kitten yawned on Bikram's lap. "Really Vinny, we shouldn't have left so quickly."

"Who cares, they give a *tamasha* every month. Next time tell Zeenat no more of those bloody jugglers." The car swerved towards a roundabout and nearly collided with a wedding procession.

"So what do you do at the embassy, Mel?" asked Arun.

"I'm at the consular's office."

"What happens in the consular's office?"

"Immigration, visas . . ."

"VISAS! Oh, my God!" The car careened round a corner and dodged another wedding procession. The groom's horse kicked and neighed and nearly unseated its passenger.

* * *

The weekly card party at Padmini's house was a social necessity. Without going there, there was no way to find out which family was on the up and which down, where the best dressed ladies were shopping, whose children had gotten into Modern School, and so forth. Ritu alternately dreaded and enjoyed the occasion. Padmini served very good food and everyone came wearing such nice things; sometimes jokes were told and the atmosphere was very entertaining. But in general, one had to pay close attention to the conversation and mind what was being said, and this effort of concentration combined with a card game taxed Ritu's energies considerably.

Several tables were arranged around the living room and the veranda. The ladies sat in groups of four, shuffling cards, eating appetizers and drinking sodas. Ritu was late, as she had taken extra care with her outfit, hoping to earn Nirmala's approval. Last week she had been harshly criticised for wearing a blouse that clashed with her sari border.

"Ritu, what has taken you so long? The game is half over. But come sit, Mrs Dasgupta just left. You can play partners with Mrs Shastri." Padmini shuffled the deck. Nirmala shot a swift, appraising glance at Ritu's blouse.

"So sorry. But lately commuting in Delhi has become such a chore. So much of traffic." Ritu assumed her place at the table and deliberately pushed back her sari to make certain that all the ladies could see her gold bangles.

"You have come by car?" asked Mrs Shastri.

"Of course."

"Did you dismiss it?' Nirmala took full measure of the bangles.

"It has just gone to fetch home the children."

"Have some pakoras." A servant unsteadily proffered a plate of appetizers. Ritu and Padmini took several.

"Do you know that Uma is now taking yoga lessons for

slimming?" said Nirmala. "Yet she refuses to restrict her diet and that is more the issue."

Ritu paused awkwardly, her pakora in mid-air. She was anxious whenever the subject of dieting came up, as she had put on quite a bit of weight since her marriage. How could she help it? Her mother-in-law was always making special Punjabi sweets and Amritsar-style parathas that were especially delicious. Fortunately, Ashok didn't seem to mind, he had also grown heavier.

"So I hear Amita is off to the US again!" Padmini sniffed as she dealt a round of cards. "You should see her house. Only American stuff. American shampoos, plastic holders, a new toaster, and a telephone without a cord. Now she calls me only when she is having her bath!"

"How can they let her go to America always?" Nirmala scowled. "It is difficult enough just to get a passport, and it is impossible for an unmarried woman to get a visa. I suppose she gets one because she works for Delta. But my sister was working for Lufthansa and she was not going to Germany day and night!"

"Perhaps she has got some boyfriend," said Mrs Shastri, looking up at Padmini for confirmation. "It is very odd that she has not been married. What is your opinion Ritu, you were school chums, no?"

Ritu fumbled with her cards, unable to think of an answer that would both satisfy Mrs Shastri and defend Amita. It was very odd that Amita was still unmarried. Ritu had admired her tremendously since their days in convent school, though in recent years she'd grown very sophisticated and reserved, which made Ritu admire her all the more. Her father was a doctor and her mother was a poet—they were Goan Christians. It occurred to Ritu that this accounted for Amita's outlook on things like marriage and travel.

"Maybe she likes to go to America because she is a Christian!"

"Humbug," snapped Nirmala. "When does she go to church here in Delhi? She is always sleeping on Sundays. I know because once I went to her flat at two in the afternoon and the servant said she was not out of bed!"

"Her action is truly peculiar." Mrs Shastri tucked a stray curl into the large bun that rested on her nape. "I couldn't get a visa to the US until I was married even though I showed them all the proof of property. Papa even came along and gave the embassy people his business card."

"She must be working for the CIA. Otherwise Delta would not have her," declared Padmini.

"But she always comes back to India," said Ritu timidly. "They are mostly afraid that an Indian girl will settle with an American husband and that she has not done."

The servant shuffled in with a tray of lime sodas. Padmini scolded him for neglecting to make her lime sweet enough and sent him back to the kitchen. He returned with a fresh drink. She took a large gulp and pressed the glass to her forehead with an anguished sigh.

"My husband, how angry he makes me!" Padmini slammed the glass on the table and rummaged through her purse in search of her *paan* box. "He neglects the household, leaving all the work to me. Always playing cricket! He thinks of nothing else."

"Are you positive that's all he thinks about?" Nirmala fished an ice cube from her drink and began to chew it. "That cricket crowd is very fast. All that exercise. And those banquet dinners at the hotels. I understand they go to discos later for dancing."

"Yes, Padmini, so much exercise, just see what it does!" said Mrs Shastri, reaching for a pakora.

"It creates a gulf. He is quite slim now but you have put on too much weight since you had Vivek," said Nirmala.

"But now I am not taking breakfast or lunch." Padmini reviewed her hand.

"Night eating is the culprit!" cried Ritu. "I read about it in *Vogue* magazine. And we ladies should take exercise if only to keep up with our husbands!"

"So Ashok is keeping up with his yoga, then?" asked Mrs Shastri.

"He takes exercise in the mornings. Sometimes the yoga master comes on Sundays and I, too, join in." This was a mild exaggeration. Ritu had tried yoga four or five times but found the postures very uncomfortable. Ashok was proud of his yoga regimen. He insisted that regular practice brought a spiritual benefit, which was why he preferred yoga to cricket.

"My niece has taken this Jane Fonda course. Such muscles she has got!" Mrs Shastri examined the pink polish on her long nails.

"After so much exercise and a few drinks a man forgets that he is married, and then what? Dancing, carrying on with whatever girl is there. When was the last time Vinod took you out dancing, Padmini?"

Ritu shuddered. Had Ashok ever been unfaithful? He was so devoted to his family, to his two children, he loved nothing more than to lie on the *bersati* and eat his mother's parathas while he and Ritu watched old films on the television. Padmini's husband, Vinod, was different. He loved clothes and colognes, he was also vain and impatient and uninterested in his wife's friends. Lately he seemed thoroughly uninterested in his wife. Padmini had been quite attractive when she was younger, but she had let herself go after her marriage. Everyone knew that Daljit, Nirmala's husband, and Vinod kept mistresses. All the men in the cricket crowd did. Ashok and Vinod were not friends, Ritu thought reassuringly, so there was no danger of Ashok adopting Vinod's habits.

"So there was another cricket banquet on Friday, yes?" Nirmala eyed Padmini.

"Thank God Vinod is taking that crew to the hotel and keeping them out of this house."

"I understand they invited that girl from the American Embassy."

"What girl?"

"The one who issues the visas."

Around the table hands ceased shuffling and arranging cards.

"The one who is always wearing slacks?" asked Mrs Shastri.

"Melanie Andrews is her name."

"Oh yes! She is the one who issues the visas! My neighbour just had an appointment with her!" cried Ritu.

"Yes, Stupid, that we know! She is known for going out with that fast crowd—Kitten Singh, Binky Kumar and that lot." Nirmala pursed her lips and adjusted the thick folds of her silk sari around her neck. "Apparently either she or some other foreign girl was carrying on with Vinod in such a way they had to leave the dance floor. There was quite a bit of drinking as well."

"Who told you this?" Padmini dug her fingernails into her elbows.

"My God, everyone has been saying it. Neelam, Ramesh . . ."

"She is quite an attractive girl, is she not?" said Ritu, insensitive to Padmini's distress. Padmini stood up quickly, knocking over her lime soda.

"Oh, shut up! Vinod is just trying to get a visa for our niece Parveen so she can go study in the US. He's only humoring that woman. And how can he keep up his business, travelling to the west and back, without keeping in good stead with the embassy?

"Daljit has done it without going to disco parties nightly," retorted Nirmala.

Ritu shook with a fresh wave of fear. The thing people did to get a visa! The stories they invented, the bribes, and then the interminable wait at the embassy, and the interview! A ghastly ordeal, having one's entire life scrutinised, plucked apart by a foreigner, no less... Ritu trembled to think of it.

"Sunil and Bipi were denied visas just last week," said Mrs Shastri. "But I have since heard that Bhupa Singh is taking his family to New York for the summer."

"I'm sure Parveen will get her visa if Vinod stays out late again this week." Nirmala lit a cigarette and flung the match on the floor. Ritu stared helplessly at her cards, wondering if the game was defunct. Padmini stormed into the kitchen to shriek at the cook who had paused for a *bidi* at an inauspicious moment.

* * *

Rakesh and Zeenat's party went on very late that night. After dancing at the Number One everyone went for a drive through Old Delhi and had breakfast at a tea stall behind the Red Fort. Melanie spent the night at Kitten's. Kitten's sister, Tippy, was a fashion designer and persuaded Melanie to purchase several *salwar-kurta* outfits. Melanie bravely decided to wear one to the office on Monday.

Melanie worked in the West Building, which was smaller and more tolerable than the Chancery, which loomed, grim and joyless, at the edge of a long row of diplomatic compounds. The most impressive feature of the American Embassy was its central air-conditioning, which never broke down, even when midsummer power shortages felled ceiling fans and air-coolers throughout the capital. It was something the ladies in South Delhi never tired of discussing.

"Good morning, Joe." Melanie said.

"Hi. Will you look at all these headaches?" Joe sorted through a stack of passports. "Summer vacation's round the corner. Everyone and his uncle will be tapping on our little window panes. Joe removed his glasses and wiped them with a fresh Kleenex. "I can feel the heat already."

"But it's only February." Melanie pushed her glasses onto her nose and pulled her hair into a pink band.

"It's murderous. You have to take salt pills and then you get high blood pressure." Joe and India were clearly unsuited for each other. His leaden skin and limp blonde hair belonged under a cold sky and between dim, quiet walls.

"What are we doing about that girl who wants to go to Chicago to visit her sister?"

"Sister? Everybody's sister is living in Chicago. I guess we're supposed to believe that 880 million Indians are living in the US right now. Of the 15,000 Indians who will visit America on tourist visas this year, guess how many will adjust their status—in other words—stay there? Over 3,000."

"But we can't prevent that, sitting here in . . ."

"Unfortunately not. But you gotta keep an eye on the unmarried ones. They're dangerous. And watch out for those green card marriages."

Melanie recalled that Kitten and Tippy had asked her about getting visas so they could spend their summer holiday in New York. She couldn't imagine that either of them would want to leave India. They were rich and happy here, how could they live in small flats, making do without the cook, the bearer and the dhobi, having to go to offices and supermarkets? In their case, Joe was wrong.

"I've got some unmarried friends whose relatives studied with me and came back to India. They've also got a lot of property. I can vouch for them."

"Are you sure?" Joe turned around, his glasses slipped off his nose.

"Yes, I can."

"You know, Melanie, you shouldn't wear that native stuff too much. It'll give people the wrong impression."

"What impression?"

"That you like it here."

"I do. I love it."

"Love it? Oh come on."

"I do. I love the people, I love the way it smells..."

"Just wait till the heat starts. You won't love it anymore." Joe turned away in a huff. Melanie sat silently for a moment, fingering the edge of her chiffon *dupatta*. It was probably not a good idea to let her co-workers know how much she was enjoying herself.

"Ritu, Ritu! The news has come! Just see!" Ashok pushed through the door, carrying a stack of documents and several boxes of sweets. The dog barked at his heels, the cook peered from the kitchen doorway to see what was going on. Ritu was stretched out on the sofa, reading the latest on the Chunky Pandey scandal in the *Filmfare*.

"Ritu, come! Oh what a day." He tossed the documents on the couch and opened the sweets.

"But Ashok, I am so tired, I cannot get up." The card party had been especially draining and her morning shopping excursion had not been a success.

Ashok knelt by her side, arms outstretched, a sweet box in each hand. "What a day, my darling! Take a *ladoo!*" He fell to his knees and held out a tinsel-covered box filled with golden sugar balls. "A treat for my sweet!"

"Babu, what is this? You have got another promotion?" Ritu turned on her side to reach the *ladoos.*

"No, no, much more! The conference has been approved! We are going to the US! Even the visas have been obtained! We fly to America in one month's time. And hotel preparations for wives are being arranged so you can also come! This *barfi* I got from Bengali market—so delicious."

Ritu considered whether she should telephone Padmini with the news or wait until the next card party when all the ladies would be assembled. Maybe it would be better to wait until she got her own visa before telling anyone.

"When do I get my visa?"

"The Head of Management will see to it. I must tell Mummyji about this." He ran upstairs to his mother's room. Ritu laid a hand against her heart. If the Head of Management arranged everything, then, perhaps, she would not have to endure the interview. She could come back with a cordless phone and a hair dryer, like the ones Amita had.

Arun Gupta's living room had an elaborate stereo system and an enormous Japanese TV and VCR. No one asked how he managed to get them past the customs without paying the huge duty fines. But his parents knew a lot of people. Arun also had Dunhill cigarettes, American Scotch whisky and French cheese, so everyone visited his house.

"I've got to go abroad at least three times a year," Arun stretched over a tussar bolster, stirring his drink. "But I could never live anywhere but in India. New York is terribly exciting for one week and then one starts to die in it. And Mel, really, your American cities have become so tacky . But such lovely discos."

"And what is wrong with our discos?" Rinku Sethi lay on the couch counting her silver bangles. "Our Number One has all the hits and it is much easier to get into."

"My friends in New York never have a problem getting in anywhere." Arun smoothed the folds of his ivory kurta over his hips. "Melanie, you're looking awfully smart in that *bandani* thing. You have already assimilated in full. You're part-Indian now. Kitten should whip up some *zardozi* thing for your embassy balls that'd really knock them out." Arun sorted through a pile of music tapes. "Who's for some Iron Butterfly?"

Rinku yawned and stretched her arms over her head. Her sari fell onto her lap, revealing a trunk of firm golden flesh between two bands of magenta silk. "Arun, please fetch me a drink," she moaned, pulling her sari over a shoulder. "So thirsty."

"Of course, darling, what'll it be? A sweet *nimbu*, perhaps?"

"But *nimbu* is so dull..." Rinku coiled strands of her magnificent black hair around her ornamented wrists. Melanie's fingers surreptitiously crept to her own meager braid, which seemed woefully inadequate. She leaned across Kitten's legs, in fitted peacock blue silk, for some cheese. Vinod sat down next to her.

"You are looking beautiful tonight," he whispered.

"Oh Vinod, you're making me very self-conscious, with all these dazzling women..."

"I must see you tomorrow. I'll take you to Tughlakabad. It's where I used to play as a boy. Old Turki ruins. Say you'll come." Melanie was supposed to go swimming at the American pool with Joe's wife, just to be polite.

"Meet me at the Imperial Hotel at 1.30."

"I..."

"You'll love it. Say Yes."

"I forgot where."

"The Imperial. 1.30."

Melanie's new chappals made an unpleasant slap as she walked through the marble lobby of the Imperial. A group of Australian tourists in shorts and hiking boots argued with a very fat Sikh taxi driver in a hot pink turban. Salesmen squinted at her; the display cases sparkled with embroidered bags, jewellery, silk scarves, ivory carvings, cloth paintings. The scent of jasmine smoke was very strong.

"You've come." Vinod leaned against a pillar, in flared slacks and an orange shirt. Melanie was startled, she had never seen him in anything but silk kurtas. He slipped his hand under her arm and led her back through the lobby out to his car, a huge white Mercedes which overwhelmed the other lowly vehicles in the lot.

"Where'd you get this car?"

"The Kuwaiti ambassador unloaded it on me before he left. He didn't want to ship it home so I swapped it for some old jewellery." He slipped a cassette into the tape player. Violins swooned, a piercing soprano divulged a plaintive tale of love. Vinod gasped and pressed his hand against his heart. "Do you know what she is singing?" he cried. "She says, 'My body burns. It is on fire, but you withhold your quenching love.' Ahh! So marvellous!" He pressed the accelerator. Bicyclists, cattle, rickshaws and scooters all yielded, Delhi's urban sprawl gradually eased into clusters of villages and grain fields and soon, Tughlakabad was visible in the distance. They drove up a steep incline, past huge, crumbling ramparts, to a place with a wide view of the fort and the fields below.

"When Mohammed of Ghazni sacked Delhi in the twelfth century, a dog bit him. He was so enraged by this that he ordered every living thing in Delhi to be killed. His soldiers set about slaughtering every animal, every child, even the birds. It took them three days." A murky haze hung in the air, huge thunderclouds moved along the horizon. Vinod gazed out at the spoiled fort and the expanse of fields and rocks stretching towards the dark ridge of clouds at the vista's edge. His eyes shone with tears; the drama of his posture, his classical features and thick waves of hair clashed with his polo shirt and polyester trousers.

"You love India, don't you?" asked Melanie.

"Love it? It is my home, my land! It is the greatest, oldest country on earth!"

"Then why do so many Indians want to leave?"

"I don't understand what you're talking about."

"In my job I meet hundreds of people who want to go live in the US. We can't issue visas for all of them, of course, but it's so hard to have to decide. I can understand those who are poor wanting to leave but the others . . ."

"Melanie, Melanie!" Vinod made Melanie sit next to him on the wall. "It is very simple. We don't have enough jobs here. That's it."

"Do you think those who leave want to return?"

"Of course! They only go for work. You have so much wealth in America, it is your duty to share it. My niece wants a visa to the US, but only to study. She'd never stay there, we wouldn't let her. My mother won't have a mixed marriage in the family." He laughed, lit his cigarette and tossed the used match on the rocks. "I've been a dozen times and I've never stayed. You should be more trusting."

"I am!"

"But that other chap is a wretch. What's his name, Lindy?"

"Joe Lindsey."

"He thinks we're all crooks. That's no way to conduct your foreign policy. Look at those fat birds. Nothing gets wasted in this country." Vinod pointed to a flock of vultures descending upon the corpse of a buffalo.

"Are you married, Vinod?"

Vinod laughed nervously. "Melanie, you've been here long enough to know that every Indian out of knee-pants is married."

"Kitten isn't."

"Well, she's young and rich. She'll be married off soon enough. Her parents will make sure to arrange a proper alliance."

"Not a love match?"

"Partially. Nowadays we get to choose among an approved set of candidates." He took Melanie's hand and pressed it against his heart. "My wife and I don't see much of each other. We lead different lives. All she wants to do is read film magazines and play bridge. Not like you."

"Are you separated?"

"Yes. Yes, we are. Especially in our minds." He laced his fingers through hers and leaned forward to kiss her. She pulled back.

"But Vinod . . ."

"What?"

"Are you . . ."

"Come here." He held her face in his hands and kissed her hard upon the mouth. A translucent orange haze spread over the sky. Vinod clenched Melanie's arms and pressed her to his chest. A wild shriek pierced the air.

"What was that?"

"Just a peacock. Don't mind it."

"Oh Vinod, look!" Several ragged children started from behind the broken wall, hushed and fascinated.

"*Arrey,* scat!" Vinod waved them away.

* * *

Ritu arrived at Padmini's wearing one of her most expensive Kanchipuram saris with a heavy gold border. She had had her hair done at the Elegant Beauty Salon in the morning with an extra lacquer twist at the back. She had also had a special pedicure and rose-cream foot massage. Nirmala, Padmini and Mrs Shastri took full notice.

"Ritu, you are looking done up for a wedding or something. What has happened?" Nirmala quickly assessed the thickness of the gold border.

"Oh, this old thing . . ." Ritu lowered herself into her chair. "I've been going through my closet, tossing out what is of no use. I must make room for the new."

"Clearly something is up. Come on Ritu*ji*, out with it!" said Padmini, shuffling a pack of cards.

Ritu felt nervous. The Kanchipuram sari was a dead giveaway. She had envisioned easing the news into the conversation after a few hands of bridge, to take everyone by surprise.

"Ashok wants me to get some new things and start wearing my better saris. It is fitting, after all."

"Fitting? Why? You are going someplace?"

"Just abroad."

"Where to?"

"We are going to America for an international hoteliers' conference, that is all." All heads in the room swerved round.

"When?"

"In one month's time. There is so much to do before that." Ritu tried to appear very calm as she sipped her lime soda.

"But surely ladies are not invited. That is quite out of form."

"In this case, wives will accompany."

"You have been given a visa and an air ticket'?"

"Of course. How else could I go?"

Nirmala was stunned. Padmini yelled for a fresh plate of pakoras. Ritu, stirred with confidence, ran a freshly manicured hand over her coiffure to let all the ladies see her gold and diamond rings.

"Have you got a six-month tourist or twelve-year multiple entry?" asked Mrs Dasgupta. Ritu paused. The five-year multiple entry was certainly the better one.

"The latter type."

"When do you go for your interview?" asked Mrs Shastri.

"There was no need. The Head of Management arranged it."

"You must be very careful. If they discover any CIA connection in this trip, Ashok will not be able to work anywhere when he returns!" said Nirmala. "With everything so prearranged it sounds like a foreign hand at work. Don't you think Padmini?"

Padmini gave Nirmala a defiant smirk. "Visas are not so hard to get. Our niece Parveen has just got one. She will be going to Texas to complete her studies."

Nirmala went pale. Padmini took the plate of pakoras from the servant and passed it to Ritu. "Ritu*bhen*, have this special *bhindi*. Perhaps you and Parveen will be travelling on the same aircraft. What is your program in the US?"

Ritu paused. There was one thing she had always wanted to see, something everyone dreamed of in convent school and at ladies college.

"We are planning to go to Disneyland," she answered firmly. Mrs Shastri gasped and Nirmala dropped her cards, exposing her hand.

* * *

Kitten's dressing table was covered with innumerable little boxes made of silver and semi-precious stones, each containing special potions for the eyes, skin and hair. Melanie watched with reverence as Kitten's fingers probed each vial and dipped wands into jewelled bowls to mix the essences. She had thought it impossible to increase Kitten's beauty, but as the rites were completed, Kitten did just that, time after time. Kitten caught a glimpse of Melanie's limp hair and freckled cheeks in the mirror. There wasn't much point in putting any make-up on her, it couldn't disguise her irredeemable bone structure and unfortunate colouring. "Gosh, Mel, you've been seeing quite a bit of Vinod, haven't you?" Kitten traced a *kajal* stick along her eyelid with expert precision.

"It's so kind of him to show me around. You grew up with all these temples and monuments but it's still amazing for me." Melanie sighed dreamily, remembering the scent of Vinod's cologne, the thickness of his hair and eyelashes.

"He's a good sport that way." Kitten smoothed coconut oil over her face. "I'm very fond of Vinod, but he's a tricky chap, Mel. All those fellows have notions about foreign girls. And he's got a wife, you know."

Melanie recalled that Vinod had been pressing her to spend a weekend in Jaipur with him. They had only kissed in ruins and gardens and in his car, though he had always struggled for more. In America, that didn't mean very much, but in here, perhaps it did.

"Aren't Vinod and his wife separated?"

"They don't spend a lot of time together, if that's what you mean. They're hardly getting a divorce, their parents wouldn't have it. We Indians don't divorce they way you people do." Kitten dabbed a small circle of brilliant pink powder on her forehead.

"Do they have children?"

"Two, I think. Their house is very pokey, she spends all her time fussing over the kids, playing cards and shopping."

"Do you think I shouldn't see him so often?"

"Do you like him?"

"Well, yes, he's awfully fun to be with . . ." Melanie thought of how handsome he looked yesterday evening when they climbed to the top of Humayan's tomb at sunset and he sang *ghazals* and nearly cried.

Kitten hummed softly as she rubbed oil on her arms and slid several glass bangles over her wrists. "He's probably interested in your power at the embassy. He needs visas for his business."

Melanie realised that she didn't know what Vinod's business was. He was elusive whenever the subject came up, though he had once said something about being an engineer.

"Isn't he involved in engineering?"

"I suppose, in a very roundabout way. He deals in armaments and high-tech stuff. That's why he has to travel. I'm hardly in the same line but I'd be very hurt if I discovered you were doling out visas to his friends without giving one to me for my summer holiday." Kitten sighed wearily as she pulled a comb through her black mane. "Really Mel, sometimes I envy you Americans with your thin hair. It's such work to manage all this." She played with it before the mirror, half annoyed to impose order on its magnificent wildness. "Do you think I should keep it out tonight or will it get in the way?"

Melanie was thinking of the six passports Vinod had given her so she could stamp five-year multiple entry visas on them.

Ashok sat cross-legged on the sofa while his mother fed him his favourite Amritsar-style parathas. The children screamed and chased each other around the room.

"Deepa, Ranjit, hush! Your father is taking his meal," Ashok shouted between bites of paratha. His mother watched with a satisfied grin.

"What is the matter with Ritu lately? A head condition?"

"No, Maji, she is feeling a case of nerves. It is due to preparing for the conference."

"Of course. It is far to go. Is the trip a must?"

"It will be a great international event. Hoteliers and travel agents from every continent will attend."

Ritu came through the door, struggling with an armload of parcels. She called for the house-boy and collapsed on the sofa with a groan. "So much of organising. Thank goodness you have done the visas and air ticket, or I would expire." Ashok went into the kitchen to get a Campa Cola.

"So daughter, Ashok has made all of the arrangements?"

"Oh yes. Ashok, have you got the visas yet?" Ritu was hoping that the passport had already been arranged and stamped so she could take it to Padmini's card party next week to show everyone. Ashok sauntered back to the sofa with his cola.

"So all the work has been completed?" Ashok's mother sprinkled salt on a paratha and passed it to her son. Ashok did not respond.

"Ashok, what is the matter?"

Ashok put his cola on the side table and thoughtfully chewed his paratha, scratched his neck and yawned. "Hoi, hoi, very nice masala . . ."

Ritu gripped the edge of the sofa. "Ashok, what has happened to my visa? Are we not going on the trip?"

Ashok pulled his right foot onto his lap and began to massage the toes. "The Head of Management is most overextended. We will have to get your visa through our own channels."

"What?" Ritu leapt to her feet. "But how? You have seen the line stretching around the embassy daily? Do you know what Neelam and Sunil endured and still they were rejected?" She sobbed and ran upstairs to the bedroom. If she skipped the card party everyone would be suspicious. If she went to the embassy for an interview, everyone would find out. A vision of Padmini's eyes and Nirmala's contemptuous smile assailed her. She threw herself on the bed and cried wildly, crumpling her new printed linen *kameez.*

* * *

Melanie repeated her questions and paid little attention to the answers. The man sitting across from her looked like he was about to faint. She handed him back his passport and told him to return in a week. They all looked so hopeful, so anxious. Were there really no jobs for these people? Did they just want to visit their relatives in Chicago or Florida? She leaned into the microphone.

"Number 406, Mr Anand Guha, to Window 3, please."

A young man stepped into the booth. Melanie peered at the application, filled in a round, cursive hand and looked up at the applicant. He was alarmingly—extraordinarily beautiful. She gaped at him for a moment, then struggled to resume control. A terrible blush rose in her cheeks as she blurted out the first question.

"Mr Guha, for what purpose do you wish to visit the United States?"

"I am a jazz musician and I would like to go to New York for further studies."

Melanie looked at his pale blue *kurta* and the string of *tulsi* beads around his neck and was quite bewildered.

"You are a jazz musician?"

"Yes. I play jazz flute."

"I see." She fumbled with his papers. "Are you—have you—performed any time recently?"

"Yes. My group is called Prakriti. We played at the Indian International Center last month. Here are the reviews." He handed her several newspaper clippings. In the photographs he sat cross-legged between a bassist and a trumpeter, wearing a long white kurta, a silver flute at his lips.

"Would this be your first trip to the United States, Mr Guha?"

"You can call me Anand."

"Anand." She repeated. She had encountered the word in a textbook of Indian studies. She stared at him, unable to proceed with the interview. "Do you mind if I ask, Mr Guha, what does Anand mean?"

"Bliss," he replied, smiling.

* * *

The days that followed were filled with doubt and torment. Ashok was very busy preparing for the conference and seemed to have no time to help Ritu with her visa arrangements. She skipped Padmini's card party, claiming to have too many errands to complete before her departure. She was prepared to give up going to Los Angeles, seeing Disneyland, the whole thing, rather than endure the interrogation required to obtain a visa. It wasn't as though she or Ashok had ever done anything wrong, no, they hadn't, they'd always lived quite correctly. Ashok earned more each year and Ritu was gaining acceptance in all the right circles and their children had been accepted at South Delhi Day School. It was just the idea of having one's life scrutinised by a complete stranger, by a foreigner, no less, that petrified her. It seemed such a violation of the privacy of one's very life. Why did they need to ask such questions? Why did one have to explain the desire to travel a bit? It was all so perplexing and disturbing.

Nonetheless, Ritu hired a special tailor to make several new *salwar* suits, in case the Head of Management got her a visa at the last minute. She decided that some new saris would also be necessary for galas or banquet dinners. Nagma Sari House was having an exhibition-cum-sale of Benaras and Kanchipuram silks, so she took the car and went down to Connaught Circus to make some purchases.

Ritu took a seat near the display area where the owner sat cross-legged, chewing on *paan* and hurling orders at the staff. He greeted Ritu warmly and sent a boy into the kitchen to bring her a cold soda. Bolts of cloth were unfurled, piles of brocade saris were unwrapped and laid out for Ritu's perusal. She examined the borders, asked to see more of the *pallus*, questioned the colour schemes, found some fault with the weaving, required heavier silk or softer tussar, a better blue or a nicer pink. The salesmen complied with each of her requests, presenting finer, richer, lovelier fabrics, until great heaps of cloth were piled all around.

Ritu was enjoying herself immensely: she loved looking at the designs, drinking sodas, being waited on and attended to. She was just preparing to make some final decisions when she heard a great clamour at the door. She looked up to see Nirmala, Mrs Dasgupta and Mrs Singh come through the front door. She gasped in horror. They would surely ask about her travel plans. But it was not possible to slip out of the store without being seen, there was only one door, and then she wouldn't have time to purchase the coral satin or the pink and green handblock.

"Heavens, Ritu, we thought you were ill when you didn't come for cards the other day. But you seem to be quite up and about." Nirmala settled her great mass onto a stool and shouted for a soda.

"We hear you're off to America. That's quite a big thing." Mrs Singh took the other stool. Mrs Dasgupta, who had a circulation problem, asked for a chair.

"You are going to the USA? Oh my!" cried Mr Patel, the head salesman. "My nephew has recently opened a motorcycle shop in Cincinnati, Ohio. Would you mind taking him one package on my behalf ?"

"Well, Ritu, have you got the visa yet?" Nirmala looked very skeptical. Ritu felt her hands trembling.

"It is in the works. Ashok is working day and night and I haven't pressed him about it. And I am so busy with my own arrangements."

"You can't be sure about these visas until they're stamped in your passport," said Mrs Singh. "Padmini has said Vinod will be getting one for her and six for his business partners but you can't be certain. The Americans are very cagey about who they allow in."

"I have visited the Republic of Oman," said Mr Patel proudly. "And Hungary and Romania also. Just see." He held out a tattered passport which bore several illegible stamps in Arabic and Roman scripts. The ladies examined them. "And one visa to Australia. Have a look." He flipped to a clean page stamped with one neat, long-expired Australian visa.

"How did you obtain this?" asked Mrs Singh.

"My cousin was employed at the Australian High Commission."

"But you did not visit Australia?" Mrs Dasgupta called from her chair.

"It was difficult to manage at the time. But the visa I did get." The ladies studied it carefully.

"So Ritu, what have you purchased?" asked Nirmala. Ritu turned to the pile of fabrics and indicated several of the more expensive selections.

"I will need many outfits for all the Los Angeles galas," Ritu answered with as much equanimity as she could summon.

"Ritu, you are acting very peculiar. Something is afoot. Has the trip been cancelled?" said Nirmala. Mrs Singh and Mrs Dasgupta looked up.

"Not at all. Why should there be a problem?" Ritu felt drops of perspiration breaking on her forehead.

Mr Patel leaned forward. "Mrs Sharma, if you are in any way able to procure an extra visa for my friend Mr Bhandari,

I will happily pay your scooter fare to the US Embassy. . . ." A group of noisy Germans came through the door, deflecting everyone's attention. Ritu grabbed her purse and ran out of the shop, leapt into her car and ordered the driver to head home as quickly as possible. She rolled up the glass windows and huddled behind her sunglasses. Somehow, someway, she had to get a visa. It was very clear that if she did not go to America, she would never be able to play cards at Padmini's again.

The Head of Management was too busy to accept phone calls. The Delta office said Amita was out of the country for at least a month. Ashok had to go to Bombay for meetings. Ritu realised, miserably, that to get a visa she would have to go to the American Embassy, fill out an application form, wait in line and be interviewed, just like everybody else.

Ritu arrived at the West Building promptly at 9 a.m. The line already stretched all the way to the Burmese Embassy. Eventually she got into the holding room where people sat on folding chairs, waiting for their name to be called. She read through five film magazines and nodded off to sleep. When her name was announced over the loudspeaker, she shrieked, and everyone in the room turned to stare at her. She trembled violently behind her sunglasses as she gathered her things and walked into the interview booth.

Joe sat behind the glass, holding her application form. "Good morning, Mrs Sharma. I understand you wish to accompany your husband to America for a convention. Your husband works for the Pleasant Travel Group, correct?"

"Yes," Ritu croaked.

"And this would be your first journey outside India, correct?"

"Yes."

"Do you have any children, Mrs Sharma?"

"One boy, one girl."

"Mrs Sharma, what kind of property do you and your husband own?"

Ritu's mind went blank. She stared at Joe helplessly.

"Mrs Sharma?"

Ritu went unconscious and crashed against the wall.

When she opened her eyes she was lying on the sofa of Melanie's office with her head in Melanie's lap.

"Mrs Sharma? Are you feeling okay?" Ritu vaguely discerned a white, angular face with pale blue eyes gazing down at her. A hand gently stroked her hair.

"Where am I?"

"You're at the American Embassy. Everything's fine. You just fell ill." Ritu heaved herself onto an elbow and looked around the room. She saw a large wooden desk with an American flag and a Thai Airways calendar on the wall. She clutched Melanie in desperation.

"Oh please, miss, please do not deny me the visa! I have no interest in settling in the US. I only want to go to Disneyland and then return home! If I do not get it how they will laugh at me!" She threw her head into Melanie's lap and sobbed hysterically.

"I'm sorry, Mrs Sharma, who will laugh at you?"

"The ladies at the card party! Mrs Shastri and Nirmala Malhotra and Padmini Bhatia! Mrs Bhatia's husband, Vinod, can get any visa at any time, but we have got no channels and no influence, and I have already told them that I am going with my husband. If I cannot play cards at Mrs Bhatia's house I will become a social ruin! Oh please, miss, please, please . . ."

As each name affixed to various unanswered questions and anxieties that had borne down on Melanie for a long while, she pulled Ritu upright, pushed her hair off her face, which was wet with tears and perspiration, and handed her a box of tissues.

"Here, Mrs Sharma. I'll approve your application at once.

You can collect your passport tomorrow at noon. And if there's anything else I can do for you, please let me know."

Ritu clutched the box of tissues and stared dumfounded at Melanie.

Melanie debated whether or not to attend the big Saturday night cricket banquet at the Taj Hotel. She imagined, dreadfully, that Vinod had boasted to everyone about the sexual and professional favours she had provided him. If word got back to the protocol officer she would be in trouble, and she was afraid that if she saw Vinod, she would yield to him, as she had so many times before. But when Arun and Kitten drove up in a car and insisted that absolutely everyone would be at the cricket banquet and it would look very peculiar if she stayed at home, her resistance faltered. With great reluctance she tied a skirt around her waist, threaded silver hoops through her ears, pulled a shawl over her shoulders, slipped her feet into chappals and got into Kitten's car.

Melanie saw Vinod at once. He was leaning against the bar, sharing jokes with his friends, slapping his thighs and taking great swallows of liquor. He was, suddenly and inexplicably, no longer attractive to her in his flared trousers and high-heeled boots. Why hadn't she noticed these things before? She remembered that she had indeed noticed them on that first day when they drove to Tughlakabad, but back then they had formed a part of the whole exotic landscape. She recalled the way he embraced her, digging his nails and teeth into her skin, and she felt very unhappy. Binky and Kitten disappeared. Melanie stood amid the crush, feeling remorse bear down on her as heavily as the loud music.

Vinod put down his drink and slung his arm around Melanie's shoulder. "Ah, you've come! Have a glass of something." Melanie was miserably uncomfortable with Vinod's arm draped proprietorially over her shoulder. She tried to edge away but her drew her closer.

"Where are you going, little girl?" He put his hand on her waist in a more visible demonstration of ownership. She was acutely aware of his friends taking it all in.

"Vinod please, not here . . ."

"Not here? It's just the regular crew . . ." Melanie caught Kiran's look, and pulled out of Vinod's grasp. She struggled through the crowd to the dance floor. Kiran pulled her into an embrace and they moved in a slow, awkward circle.

"Why aren't you dancing with Vinod?"

"Because I'd rather not."

He pressed his lips against her ear. "If I take you home, will you get me a visa too?" Melanie jerked away, Kiran glared at her. She wrenched out of his arms and headed towards the door.

"What's all this carrying on?" Vinod stopped her.

"Please, please don't!" She didn't want to be so close to him, to inhale his cologne or meet his eyes.

"What's got into you? Snap out of it, everyone's looking."

"I'm sorry Vinod, but . . ." Melanie stuttered, "I didn't realise that you're still living with your wife."

"What difference does that make? Marriage doesn't stop you Americans from doing what you please."

At the very moment when she wanted to appear calm and unmoved, Melanie started to cry.

"What is it? Why are you sad?" Vinod's cheeks flushed with concern as he took her by the shoulders. She felt his enormous physical strength and cowered.

"Vinod, I'm sorry, but I can't get those visas for you!" Melanie wrenched free and ran down the stairs, past the bellboys and doormen in colonial regalia, past the confused swarm of cars and guests, onto the wide street rimmed with lights and trees and towards the benign darkness of Lodi Gardens. She made her way through the wood, tears clouded her vision, her chappals slid on the mud. She scanned the skyline for sight of one of the old tombs which rose intermittently from the rim of jungle, but saw nothing except branches swishing in the breeze. She touched her Gujarati skirt and her shawl and thought of how marvellous they made her feel. She fell to her knees and wept.

After several minutes she realised that her legs were covered with mud and she was shivering. She wanted to find someone who didn't know Kitten and Vinod and Kiran. She remembered Mr Guha, the jazz musician, telling her that he lived with his mother in Jor Bagh, which was next to the park. She crossed Lodi Road and went from house to house till she found a sign that read "Guha 6/B-45". The chowkidar was fast asleep on the step. She went around the back and saw a man standing before an icon, singing and tapping out a rhythm with two brass cymbals. The man knelt before the image, placed the cymbals aside, picked up a tray of flower petals and began to trace a pattern on the earth. Melanie leaned closer and slipped in the mud.

"I'm sorry, I'm really, really sorry..."

"Miss Andrews!"

"I'm interrupting you..."

"Not at all, come sit here."

"If you're doing something private I'll go, really..."

"No, no, I was doing puja for Goddess Durga. It's Navaratri."

Wind struck the flames, Anand cupped them protectively. He looked even more beautiful in the candlelight, his smile was wonderfully consoling. "We're in Kaliyuga now, all the Gods are sleeping and can't hear any prayers, except for the Mother. There's a Navaratri mela at Kalkaji *mandir* starting from tonight. Do you want to see it?"

"Yes..."

"Let's go." He took her hand and they rose in unison. They flagged a three-wheeled scooter on the road and drove past rows of white bungalows, squatters, encampments, luxury hotels, heaps of garbage, silent herds of cows, till the spires of Kalkaji temple appeared on a hill.

The path to the temple was lined with stalls selling jewellery, coloured powders, religious pictures, necklaces and plastic and clay icons. At the temple gateway, Anand went to buy puja baskets. Melanie's eyes passed over the heaps of roses, marigolds, jasmine, tinsel, over the ripe limbs of the merchants, across the quilted canopies suspended from trees, to a row of pictures hanging in a crooked line above a tea stall. She always liked the little religious pictures that hung in every Indian home and shop—the ones where the gods had those sweet, childlike expressions—but here, a black-skinned goddess spouting blood and wielding a sword and noose stood on a corpse. Beside her was another dark goddess with fangs and withered breasts drinking the blood of her own severed head.

"Shall we go in?" Anand held two large baskets with garlands, powder and clay lanterns.

"Who's that?" Melanie pointed to the goddess.

"Chinamasta, Chamunda and Kali, whom we're going to worship now. This is her temple."

"This?"

"Yes." They left their shoes with a crippled woman and pushed their way into the temple. Worshippers clung to the railing, wailing and sobbing. Hands reached up to touch the spray of holy water. Chants blared from a loudspeaker. Melanie felt something crash against her feet. An old man rubbed his face into the ground, sobbing and muttering prayers. Anand handed Melanie's basket to the nearest priest. He threw the flowers toward the idol and flung a pail of milk over the crowd. Melanie couldn't see what the idol was. She grasped the rail and hoisted herself up. It was nothing but a huge, bulbous rock painted orange, with two narrow, feral eyes affixed to it. She turned and saw hundreds of lips moving in prayer, hundreds of eyes gazing with adoration. Anand fell to his knees. Melanie felt her hands slipping from the rail, the heavy odour of sour milk and rose petals filled her nostrils, a convulsive chant rose from the crowd. Bodies crushed her against the railing as she felt her legs and arms slacken and give way.

* * *

Kitten rested on the sofa while her old *aiya* vigorously rubbed her legs and ankles with oil. Zeenat called from the hallway.

"Kitten*ji*, where are you?"

"Here in the bedroom. Dapu's just pressing my feet." Zeenat kicked off her embroidered chappals and dropped her golden *dupatta* on the sofa next to Kitten.

"Lovely colours today, Zeenie. But you're looking awfully tired. Want a coffee?"

"No thanks. It is such a problem getting ready for the holidays. By the way, you are still friendly with Melanie, aren't you?"

"She did get me a visa before she left. Tippy and I are off to New York next week."

"I was hoping she could arrange one for our *aiya*. I just can't go abroad without taking her for the kids."

"Darling, why didn't you ask me before? Melanie's gone!"

"Gone? Already they've transferred her?"

"Didn't you hear? She quit her post and ran off to Darjeeling with a musician."

"A musician? What sort?"

"Some flute player from that group that Deepak was so mad about. Can you imagine? Her parents must be going through the roof."

Zeenat sighed and laced her fingers through her hair. "I should've asked her sooner. Maybe Vinod can help."

"I hear he's in a lot of trouble. He promised visas to his associates and didn't get them, so that deal is off. Dapu*ji*, that's enough, thanks." Kitten curled her legs under her hips and sat up. The *aiya* gathered her oil and towels and withdrew in silence.

"Rakesh bumped into him at the Oberoi and said he was with another girl from the Canadian High Commission. How can Padmini stand it?"

"God knows. He's been promising to take her abroad with him for two years but when the time comes, he's off on his own. Apparently Padmini's furious because some friend of hers got a visa from Melanie and is now in Los Angeles and she can't get anything but Hong Kong this year."

"Who went to Los Angeles?"

Kitten dabbed silver polish on her toenails. "I think it was a Mrs Sharma."

"Mrs Sharma? Who is she?"

* * *

It was more glorious than she had imagined it. The sky was a brilliant blue, a ring of mountains rose upon the horizon, the rides and the panoramas and the restaurants exceeded every expectation. Already she had seen the Pirates of the Caribbean, the Singing Bears of Frontierland and the Flying Teacups. She clutched her cotton candy and positioned herself between Donald Duck and Minnie Mouse.

"Ashok! Just take this photo!"

Ashok clicked the shutter and beamed proudly at Ritu. Her sari flapped wildly in the wind.

"Ritu, take the camera. It's my turn!" Ritu peered through the lens and framed Ashok, standing very stern and erect, between Donald Duck and Minnie Mouse, with Sleeping Beauty's Castle rising behind them.

Paying Guest

MRS MEHTA STARTED GETTING MIGRAINE headaches when she realised that for months her son Amrit hadn't been painting in his room; he was playing disco tapes and rehearsing dances before a full-length mirror. Amrit's protracted retreat had turned into a minor neighbourhood scandal; during bridge games at the Panchsheel Club, Meena Ahuja boasted of her son's triumphs in business school in Philadelphia and Simi Mahajan produced an advance copy of *Femina* magazine with a four-page article about her son Mithun, the clothing designer, and his new boutique in Hauz Khas village. The ladies then asked Mrs Mehta when Amrit was having his exhibition. She saw the way they glanced at one another, and realised they had moved past skepticism to cynicism.

The embarrassment of that particular afternoon replayed mercilessly in Mrs Mehta's mind as she lay in bed with a compress to her forehead while Gulabi, her *aiya* of thirty years, pounded her feet with ayurvedic oil. Mrs Mehta realised that something had to be done, if only to have an answer for guests and neighbours. Which was how Basu Lal moved into the second-floor bedroom.

At the age of fourteen Amrit had produced a series of remarkable paintings. Two of his drawings were printed in a literary magazine, one was displayed at the Triveni Gallery.

When Amrit's friends were applying to colleges and technical schools, Mrs Mehta arranged for Amrit to go to the National Institute of Design in Ahmedabad. Mrs Mehta was triumphant, the neighbours were jealous. But Amrit dropped out after four weeks, which created problems with Mrs Mehta's cousin upon whom severe pressure had been levied to get Amrit admitted.

Amrit went first to his cousin's house in Almora, and then back to his home in Delhi. Mrs Mehta believed it was his right to stay at his parents' house. It was very strange the way Americans tossed out their children at the age of eighteen or twenty-one and made them live in small apartments. No wonder the children then married whomever they liked and allowed their parents such little time with their grandchildren. Nevertheless, Mrs Mehta wondered if the American system gave parents an advantage, especially with a child as stubborn as Amrit.

At Diwali, Amrit produced a beautiful painting of one of the Lodi tombs, which gave Mrs Mehta hope, but then he insisted that each painting required so much work that he needed to rest for several weeks afterwards. He refused to sell anything, not even pencil sketches; so the canvas remained on display upon the piano. The piano was another symbol of Amrit's obstinacy; when other children were taking lessons in tabla or sitar, Amrit insisted on learning the piano. Mrs Mehta hunted through various embassies for a teacher and finally found a Scottish woman who lived near Old Delhi. She also found a second-hand piano in Connaught Place which was set up in the living room. Amrit learned to play three pieces: a Bach invention, a waltz and a boogie-woogie jazz song. But then his interest inexplicably waned; he said he didn't need to learn anymore, it might strain his finger muscles which he needed for painting. Mrs Mehta still made her bearer Gurumukh dust the piano so no one would suspect that it was never used.

It was at a reception for Bengali artists at the Indian International Center where Mrs Mehta saw Basu Lal in his amber-coloured silk kurta, white dhoti, necklace of *tulsi* beads and white shawl. Mrs Mehta hastened to study his paintings—mythological scenes in delicate pen and ink and watercolour, and his resume—which listed exhibits in Calcutta, Madras, Hyderabad, Kuwait and Finland. He met all her standards of how a Bengali artist should appear: hazel eyes shielded by round wire-rimmed spectacles, white hair which rolled to his shoulders, two gold pins in his earlobes. He resembled Mrs Mehta's college idol, Amar Sen Gupta who wrote poetry and played drums in a jazz band. Amar Sen Gupta had composed a love poem to Mrs Mehta which she still preserved among her most treasured possessions, even though she did not read Bengali.

When Mrs Mehta told Basu Lal that her son was an artist, he gasped and nodded gravely, as if to imply that having a son who was an artist was the greatest of blessings and responsibilities. He asked to see Amrit's work. Mrs Mehta invited him for tea. Basu Lal led Amrit into the garden where they stood under the mango tree. The image of Amrit leaning against the tree and Basu Lal's dhoti and shawl swelling in a breeze aroused such potent images of the guru and disciple that Mrs Mehta summoned a few tears. Amrit had always required special treatment, he needed a guru not a university, and so Mrs Mehta invited Basu Lal to move into the house to give Amrit art tutorials.

For several weeks, Mrs Mehta basked in glory while Simi Mahajan and the ladies from the Panchscheel Club kept stopping by to peer at the celebrated painter who had come to nurture his gifted pupil. Basu Lal was invited to tea parties, dinners and weddings. He was even profiled by columnists in various newspapers. But after the fifteenth or sixteenth tea party, Mrs Mehta observed that Basu Lal repeated his hoary lines, as though regurgitating from a script. When asked where he was from and where he'd studied, he replied, "I'm from this planet. I belong to the whole of mankind. I am a student of the whole of human experience." Mrs Mehta later discerned, through studying his sheets of biodata (he had several), that he'd lived in Nagpur, Bhopal, Calcutta and Helsinki, which still yielded few clues to his upbringing. She suspected that his father had been in the military or the railroads, which accounted for his sense of belonging to the whole of India (she discounted his claim of belonging to the whole of mankind).

Basu Lal had many annoying habits which he made no effort to restrain. He harassed Gurumukh about his laundry, he wanted his dhotis ironed with a specific amount of starch. He never spent less than two hours at breakfast; he read every newspaper and watched the news on BBC World Service and Doordarshan. He had a huge appetite and never failed to appear at every lunch, tea and dinner, sitting on the sofa and probing the nut bowl with his long fastidiously manicured fingers, sending Gurumukh to the kitchen for lime sodas without sugar or ice cubes. After several weeks of this Mrs Mehta began to wonder what was going on upstairs, other than asking Gurumukh to bring parathas and drinks. Amrit insisted that he was doing a series on the Purana College and Hauz Khas tombs and needed extra money to get the work ready in time for a winter exhibition. But neither Amrit nor Basu Lal seemed to be doing little else but taking long walks, spending hours in their rooms playing classical Indian music and jazz on the cassette player. She asked to see some of their work. Basu Lal showed her some sketches, which she remembered from the portfolio she had seen at the Indian International Center. Amrit didn't even bother to respond; he went upstairs and put on a Bee Gees' tape, turned up very loud.

After six months Mrs Mehta feared that Basu Lal was a preposterous fake. She suspected that he had stolen the paintings from someone's wall, and that he was actually a Marwari or a Punjabi who had acquired the mannerisms and costume of a Bengali artist—the ponderous gestures, the serene half smile, the raw-silk kurta and dhoti, the wire-rimmed glasses—to exploit credulous parents and art lovers. He showed no sign of either leaving or directing Amrit's education. Mrs Mehta was determined to throw him out.

But everything went awry on account of Mrs Mahajan's new paying guest.

Mrs Mehta took four aspirins, patted a cold towel over her head and marched into the dining room where she expected to find Basu Lal and Amrit with their feet on the table, reading newspapers and eating *samosas.* The room was empty, the entire ground floor was empty. Mrs Mehta heard footsteps upstairs. She ascended the stairs slowly, her ankles hurt, and found Gurumukh putting away laundry. She went onto the *bersati* to watch the sunset, and to see if they were in the backyard, playing croquet.

"Kusum! Come have a drink with us!"

Mrs Mehta peered towards the Mahajans' garden and saw Mithun, Basu Lal, Amrit and Mrs Mahajan sitting on the patio.

"In fact, why don't you all stay for dinner. It's just home food, come and join."

"We await your presence," Basu Lal grinned officiously, and patted his tussar shawl over his left shoulder. Jostled between revulsion and curiosity, Mrs Mehta ascended the stairs to put on a fresh silk sari. For many years, a fierce rivalry had consumed Mrs Mehta and Mrs Mahajan. They were both from Lahore, they had attended the same ladies college and both considered themselves aesthetes. When Mrs Mahajan disdained floral prints and started wearing Orissa handlooms, Mrs Mehta got rid of her polyester suits and appeared only in Maheswari saris. When Mrs Mahajan had a designer create a Gujarati *haveli* for her living room with antique wooden doors, brass pots and embroidered pillows,

Mrs Mehta found a designer to transform her living room into a Rajasthani fantasy, with *bandani* cushions and wood carvings. When Mrs Mahajan became vegetarian, Mrs Mehta trained herself to forgo meat (in public). But the fiercest competition was played out over their two sons. In school Mithun had reading trouble and hated boys' sports and preferred to play with his sister's dolls and clothes, which alarmed his father, the deceased Mr Mahajan, who had been equally large and slow. When Amrit ascended to fame with his art work, Mithun was failing exams. But after Amrit's inglorious departure from NID, Mithun went to design school in London and returned two years later, borrowed money from an uncle, started designing clothes and within months became one of Delhi's top designers. Mrs Mehta didn't think much of his satin miniskirts and spangled jackets, but all the daughters and sons of her friends did, and paid huge sums of money for them. Mithun bought a new Maruti, was profiled in all the magazines and invited to film star parties in Bombay while Amrit slept later and took longer lunches and read more James Bond novels.

There was an attractive new *dhurrie* in Mrs Mahajan's living room, but too many silver trays and china on the sideboard, Mrs Mehta noted with pleasure. Mrs Mahajan looked alarmingly chic in a black chiffon pant suit, her jet black hair coiled on top of her head, a simple gold chain around her neck. Everyone suspected that Mrs Mahajan had had a nose job done three years ago after a mysterious absence during which she claimed to have studied dance in New York city, for when she returned, a distinctive bump was missing. Over the years Mrs Mahajan's looks improved as Mrs Mehta's wilted. Mrs Mehta maintained a high standard with her manicure and pedicure but didn't bother to dye her hair until almost an inch of grey roots showed, nor did she manage to control her increasing weight, whereas Mrs Mahajan had a yoga instructor named Vishwas who came to the house—a shockingly handsome young man with long hair, white kurta-pyjama and *rudraksha* beads and an utterly humorless manner. The three-times-a-week, two-hour yoga lessons in Mrs Mahajan's bedroom provoked scurrilous talk but Mrs Mahajan became slim and graceful; her skin glowed and she even stopped wearing reading glasses, as a result of yogic eye exercises, she claimed.

"So Simi, what is the occasion?" Mrs Mehta lowered herself onto Mrs Mahajan's new Gujarati cushions while assessing the probable cost of the new *dhurrie.*

"You must meet with Ana, our new paying guest. She's just arrived from New York." Mrs Mehta relaxed, so this little display was just about the paying guest. Mrs Mahajan rented out the third-floor bedroom, usually to students from Bombay or Hyderabad who were connected to the family in some circuitous way. She'd only had one foreigner, Vassily, a Russian student of Tibetan *tanka* painting who had severe acne. Futile attempts to ignite a friendship between Vassily and Amrit, the two artists, died out after a few awkward tea parties in the Mahajan and Mehta living rooms, and were eclipsed by the arrival of Basu Lal. Mrs Mehta was reaching for a pakora when she saw Ana, the new paying guest, lower herself into a chair beside Mithun. She had long, dark hair, green eyes and gold skin. She was far more attractive than most Western girls who came to Delhi. She was, in fact, undeniably beautiful, poised, sophisticated—a definite coup for Mrs Mahajan.

"So Ana, what brings you to our India?" Mrs Mehta noticed an absence of wrinkles around Mrs Mahajan's chin and eyes, which confirmed the rumour of a facelift.

"Ana's here studying music."

"How nice."

"And what kind of musical pursuit would it be?" asked Basu Lal.

"Hindustani classical vocal."

Basu Lal affected great astonishment. "And do you speak our Hindi?" Mrs Mehta flinched at the word "our", since he was putatively a Bengali.

"I studied with a tutor in New York."

"Shall we have our dinner?" Mrs Mahajan sauntered towards the dining room, and motioned to the bearer to adjust the volume of the Hari Prasad Chaurasia tape on the stereo. Dapu, the *aiya,* came out from the kitchen with Mrs Mahajan's ayurvedic juice. Dapu was no more than four feet five inches high, her mouth was fixed in a perpetual scowl, her body smelled of *paan* and turmeric, her gnarled hands and feet were encased in silver bangles and anklets, gifts from Mrs Mahajan. She slid the juice in front of Mrs Mahajan and shot murderous glares at Ana and Mrs Mehta.

"Simi, you're not eating?" Mrs Mehta frowned.

"Today I'm keeping my fast for Santoshi Ma."

"What for?"

"Peace of mind, naturally."

This would normally have prompted a sermon from Basu Lal but he was abnormally silent, which was a relief—none of his pompous talk about a lotus rising out of the dung of contemporary culture . . . He could not take his eyes off Ana. Mrs Mehta noticed that Amrit was also transfixed by her. Ana, however, paid no attention to either of them, she ate her rice and dal with lowered eyes.

"Simi, I haven't heard you sing in a long time." Mrs Mehta smiled harshly and turned to Ana. "Simi created quite a stir in the ladies' college in a production of 'Hello Dolly'."

"It was so long ago I've forgotten all the words," Mrs Mahajan demurred.

"Mataji, we implore you . . ." crooned Basu Lal.

"Really, I can't."

"Then sing the *ghazal* you sang at Manju's wedding. Ana would love it." Mithun smiled at Ana, who blushed and fingered her *roti.*

"You've talked me into it." Mrs Mahajan cleared her throat and began to sing. Her voice collapsed on the high and low notes, but Mithun and Basu Lal sighed and swayed their heads and clapped vigorously when she finished.

"Such a sweet voice." Mrs Mehta dropped three sugar cubes in her tea.

"Now let's have a song from Ana. Ana, won't you?"

"Mummy, don't make her..."

"But she sings so beautifully. The Mehtas must hear her." Mrs Mahajan smiled imperiously at the girl, who blushed deeper and stared into her plate. Mrs Mahajan murmured instructions to Dapu, who took the *tanpura* out from it's dust cover and handed it to Ana. Ana sat on the floor, placed the *tanpura* on her lap and began to sing. Her voice was beautifully clear, her pronunciation of the Hindi syllables was perfect. Mrs Mehta was alarmed, this little girl made Basu Lal look like the ludicrous oaf that he was.

"Isn't she the loveliest thing?" Mithun nudged Mrs Mehta, "I want her to model for me."

When they arrived back home, Amrit and Basu Lal went straight upstairs. Mrs Mehta was both relieved and irritated that the confrontation with Amrit had been postponed. She lay in bed with a box of *gulab jamuns* to console her anxiety about Ana.

Amrit immediately went to work on a series of drawings on the Hauz Khas tombs, and inexplicably started practising the piano again. Basu Lal also started painting furiously. Mrs Mehta couldn't complain, but this burst of creativity suggested that Basu Lal was not leaving any time soon.

Neither Basu Lal nor Amrit spent very much time at home, they were always over at the Mahajans or out painting.

Mrs Mehta returned late from the Panchsheel Club. Ana, Amrit and Basu Lal were having drinks in the living room. Ana studied Amrit's painting of the Humayan's tomb displayed over the piano. It was the painting that had made his reputation, that had appeared in the literary magazine and attracted the art dealer.

"Amrit is a very promising pupil," Basu Lal proclaimed.

"Amrit executed that when he was only fourteen," Mrs Mehta glared at Basu Lal.

"Fourteen! That's amazing . . ."

Amrit blushed violently. Mrs Mehta was delighted to see the extreme discomfort on Basu Lal's face.

"Why don't you take Ana upstairs and show her your portfolio?" said Mrs Mehta. Amrit eagerly led Ana upstairs. Mrs Mehta saw Basu Lal stand up and immediately intervened.

"Basu, I . . . we must discuss your work. I am wondering what you have planned for Amrit's training."

"Ah, well, I—I have my notes upstairs . . ."

"I have so little time to read. Why don't you just tell me."

"Well, I was thinking of . . . a series on Indian musicians. I was thinking of beginning with Ana."

"But she is a foreign guest."

"But she understands the essence of raga!"

Mrs Mehta's attention was deflected by laughter and footsteps on the second floor. Basu Lal bounded up the stairs.

Mrs Mehta had never paid much attention to what Gurumukh said or did, but now she noticed that he spent a lot of time over at the Mahajans, just like Amrit and Basu Lal. He and Dapu leaned over the fence, Dapu pointed to Ana's room, held her sari over her mouth and whispered conspiratorially. Gurumukh stopped slouching and actually looked people in the eye. All of this signalled that something was happening in the upstairs rooms.

Mrs Mehta's cousin was getting married. There was a party, but Amrit refused to attend because Ana was modelling in Mithun's fashion show at the Maurya Sheraton. The second row had a troika in caftans—the wives of the Australian, New Zealand and British high commissioners. Mrs Mehta knew one of them, Mrs Carrington, because she once tried to buy Amrit's piano. But selling it would alert the neighbours to the fact that it was never used, so the offer was rejected and the piano continued to occupy the best corner of the living room which Mrs Mehta wanted for a new couch she had dreamed of when she saw it on display at the Himachal Trade Fair at the Ashoka Hotel. Mrs Mehta nodded at Mrs Carrington who waved and smiled. They almost spoke when a woman crossed Mrs Mehta's vision—a woman in a lime green sari with a great cone of lacquered black hair, pointed brows and vermilion nails which probed little vials of *paan* and *atar* and settled and resettled pearl and gold chains around her neck. She sat beside a very handsome man in a tight, cream-coloured *achkan*.

While studying his emerald and ruby rings, Mrs Mehta realised, in utter amazement, that he was Zafir Khan, the film star. The lights dimmed, music swelled and smoke machines ignited. Ana stepped from behind the curtain, radiantly ingenuous in a simple chiffon kurta, a departure from the leather and spangles upon which Mithun had built his reputation. She glided down the runway, turned and guided back to the curtain. A stream of models followed, none as beautiful as Ana. Ana appeared again, in a white skirt and choli. Mrs Mehta heard people asking questions about her while Mrs Mahajan applauded loudly. Mrs Mehta felt her stomach turning precipitously, a foreboding of an inauspicious consequence. She pushed herself onto her feet and fled through the back door.

Mithun had hired *qawali* singers for the party afterwards, with the idea that they could have an improvisation session with the disco band. The musicians reeked of whisky and hashish, their eyes were bloodshot, they didn't seem to want to sing, they said they were tired and needed to rest—

which suited the deejay, who played disco *bhangra*. Mithun, Ana and Amrit pushed their way into the discotheque, the crowd cheered Mithun. Amrit wanted to take Ana to the dance floor, but Mithun steered them to a table.

"Ana, Amrit, this is Zafir." Before Amrit was able to intervene, Mithun maneuvered Ana into a seat next to Zafir, who stared at her over a cigarette. Ana smiled and slid her hair over her left shoulder, Amrit noticed, while Zafir encircled Ana with his hands and cigarette smoke.

Mithun pulled everyone up to dance. Zafir had his arms around Ana's waist. Her choli had come undone at the back, which drew a chilly look from the woman in the lime green sari who danced with Mithun, who was too drunk to notice what was going on. The deejay played Amrit's favourite bhangra remix. Amrit pulled off his jacket and steadied himself to present his dance piece, hoping to impress Ana, Zafir and the other film stars, models and designers. He was about to execute a floor spin when Ana grabbed his arm.

"Amrit, please take me away from here." Amrit was not quite prepared to exploit the magnitude of this opportunity with Ana; he desperately wanted to display the choreography he had practiced in his bedroom for months. But Ana was already pulling him through the crowd, into a taxi, which she directed to Green Park, to the Tughlak tomb behind the market. They climbed up the stairs to the parapet under the dome. Ana wound her arm around Amrit's waist, he attempted to calm his breathing which seemed dreadfully loud.

"Mithun said this place is haunted."

"I never heard that."

"He said Delhi was filled with the ghosts of the thousands of people killed by the Lodi and Tughlak invaders." Ana leaned over the parapet and breathed the wet vapours of soil and bark rising from the garden. Amrit tried to imagine Delhi charred and slaughtered but he could only think of gardens, poets and dance parties. He wondered if she was sending him a coded erotic message of some kind, though she seemed engrossed in the garden, unaware that her choli was untied and beginning to slip off her shoulders. Ana suddenly wound her arms around Amrit's neck and shuddered into his shoulder. "I'm so glad you took me away from there."

"Me too, I hated it!" Amrit declared, though he still burned with disappointment at having been denied the chance to show off his new dance steps.

"I didn't like those men. I like being with you, just you," Ana whispered. Amrit put his arms around her as they leaned back against the stone. He kissed her forehead, her cheeks, her lips, and slid his hand under her choli. He was amazed that she offered no resistance, in fact, she was encouraging him. She didn't seem to hear the bats flapping in the dome, maybe she didn't know they were bats. Amrit tried to ignore them as he fumbled with the rest of her clothes. She grasped him by the hair, it was happening so quickly he didn't quite realise that they were making love. He felt stones and dirt crush into his back, while Ana kissed his neck and face and ran her hands down his arms.

They lay beside the parapet and ebbed in and out of dreams. The evening appeared in fragments: the fashion show, the discotheque, Ana's arms and hair. Amrit felt water on his face and opened his eyes. Rain fell from low clouds. Amrit, and Ana's arms and legs were coated with mud, the folds of their clothes were damp. This was what he had dreamed about, this was the only thing he really wanted, this and a large, quiet room with a large stereo and an air-conditioner.

Amrit paced back and forth on the *bersati*. Ana's window was shut, the yoga teacher's motorcycle was in the driveway. He had to go see Ana. Mrs Mehta rarely went upstairs due to her bad ankles. But she kept her bedroom door ajar so she could see who came and went, and Amrit had to go past her room when he went in and out. He jumped over the fence to the Mahajans' house and knocked on the door. Dapu said Ana was resting and wouldn't let him up the stairs. Amrit went to Mithun's room. Mithun was lying under blankets, with all the curtains drawn.

"I'm trying to sleep," Mithun moaned from under a pillow.

"Is Ana awake?"

"Go ask Ana."

"Dapu won't let me go upstairs."

"To hell with her, just go."

"She won't let me."

"Tell her to get me some coffee, then go."

Once Dapu was inside the kitchen, Amrit raced upstairs and knocked on Ana's door. He knocked again and waited, then tried the door, which opened. Ana was in bed, her lovely hair covering her face and her naked shoulders. Amrit knelt down and handed her his painting of Humayun's Tomb.

"You can't give this away," she smiled, admiring the painting, and casually stroking his hand. He tried not to look at her breasts, which pressed against the bedsheet.

"I want you to have it."

"Oh gosh, you're so sweet . . ." Ana slid her arms around his neck and kissed him. Amrit was conscious of the unlocked door and Dapu lurking in the hallway, though he calculated that Mrs Mahajan was occupied with the yoga teacher and Mithun wasn't going to get up any time soon. Ana unbuttoned his shirt, he fumbled with her clothes.

"Amrit, did you make plans for us to go to the mountains? You promised!"

"I will, I will, my cousin has a house, I'll . . ."

"Miss Ana, telefun . . ." Dapu's head came through the door. Amrit shouted at her to get out, which she did, but not before she'd taken a lengthy appraisal of the two of them on the bed. When Amrit came down, Dapu glared at him. He wondered whether to hand her some baksheesh or snarl at her, but she pushed him out and slammed the door shut.

Amrit spent several hours trying to get his cousin on the phone and ask his permission to use the house in Almora. When he went over to the Mahajans' in the late afternoon, Mrs Mahajan told him that Ana wasn't there. He flagged a scooter and went down to Triveni, but the building was closed. He wandered around Connaught Place, then went to the Taj Hotel. To his horror he saw Ana coming out of the Coffee Shop with the two men from the fashion show party. He trailed them down the hall, they got into a taxi. And of all people, Basu Lal got in with them.

Mrs Mehta lay in bed reading *Filmfare*. She wanted another drink and called for Gurumukh. He didn't answer, she called him four times, still there was no answer. She stood up—her ankles were swollen—and went into the kitchen but his little stool was vacant and the fan was off. She heard scuffling upstairs, and decided, despite her ankles, to see what was going on. She mounted the steps, groaning, heaving herself forward with the aid of the bannister, and finally reached the second floor. Basu Lal's door was ajar. She bristled at the sight of his precious Bengali dhotis and kurtas and his boxes of painting supplies. She saw Gurumukh hunched over a drawer, leafing through a notebook. Gurumukh's eyes were glazed with awe. When he saw Mrs Mehta he dropped the book and fled.

Mrs Mehta saw a pencil sketch of a nude woman lying across a bed. There were, in fact, a great many such sketches, some were alarmingly provocative. Mrs Mehta understood the study of anatomy was part of an artist's training, but presumably Basu Lal was no longer training, and the pictures were not mere anatomical studies. And the model, she realised, was Ana. Her immediate reaction was to throw the pictures and the man who had made them out of the house. She clutched the notebook and veered down the stairs, realising that first she had to confront Mrs Mahajan about the licentious morals of her paying guest. But Basu Lal was as much if not more at fault. She sat down. She would decide in the morning.

She locked the notebook in the godown with her jewellery and chocolate bars, took a tranquilliser and slept for ten hours.

When she awoke she heard shuffles and murmurs in the hallway. She could never leap out of bed, and twenty minutes later she emerged in a robe. She saw in horror that the picture of Humayun's Tomb was gone. She just knew it must have gone to Ana. Gurumukh handed her a note, from Basu Lal.

> To *Srimati* Kusum*ji*,
>
> I regret to pen this in haste, however the muse compels me to take hasty action in her pursuit. I feel that Amrit's education has reached a saturation point, at which he should do some contemplative reflection on his dharma-duty to Goddess Saraswati. Mrs Mahajan has asked me to assist in the reorganisation of her craft collection, and I feel that an absence from your house would be more to Amrit's benefit than deficit at this time, since it is my dharma-duty to safeguard his cultural evolution. I shall be close at hand to advise and consult on the cultivation of his artistic God-gift. I may be contacted regularly at 6/3-1 Hauz Khas, abode of *Srimati* Simi Mahajan. God blessings to thee, *Mataji* Kusum, Basu Lal.
>
> P.S. Please give instructions to Gurumukh to transfer my laundry to the Mahajan house when he has finished the job.

Mrs Mehta armed herself with a new Maheswari sari and two new antique silver bracelets and marched across the drive to demand that Amrit's painting of Humayun's Tomb be returned at once. She rang the bell. Dapu opened the door, she headed straight for the living room, and saw, to her dismay, Basu Lal drinking tea. Mrs Mahajan sauntered from the bedroom, followed by Vishwath, the yoga teacher. Vishwath held a cup of lemonade, into which he sprinkled salt. He glared coldly at Mrs Mehta, who moved her sari further down her arm to conceal her waistline.

"Kusum, is milk on your diet or not, I can't remember?"

"Just some hot tea, please. I'm sorry to bring this up, but I think there's been some misunderstanding. Amrit left one of his paintings here and we need it because there's a prospective buyer."

"Oh, really? And who's the buyer?" Mrs Mahajan nodded at Basu Lal, who nodded back with a conspiratorial grin. Mrs Mehta's heart and soul flooded with fresh hatred for him.

"Someone from out of town. Can I just fetch the painting from Ana's room?"

"Ana's not here, why don't you wait until she comes back."

"I'm short of time..."

Mithun came in the front door. "Mummy, is Ana back?"

"Everyone wants Ana today. No, she isn't."

"We're shooting tonight, she didn't show up for fittings."

The phone rang, Mithun yelled for the dhobi. Mrs Mehta was very uncomfortable, Basu Lal seemed very relaxed. Finally Mrs Mehta stood up.

"I must have the painting back, now."

"But Ana's not here and I think she locked her room. Can't you have it in the morning?" Mithun and Basu Lal went into the kitchen finally. Mrs Mehta got Mrs Mahajan alone.

"Simi, your guest has been a very negative influence."

"Oh? He was your guest for nearly a year."

"I mean Ana."

"And what is the matter with Ana? Such a sweet girl, and so talented. Amrit is very keen on her."

"She... she has modelled... without clothes!"

"That's what happens in art schools."

"Of course, I know that, but this is different!"

When Amrit arrived home late and agitated, unable to find Ana, he saw the sketchbook on the dining room table. It was unmistakably Ana, for now he had seen her without her clothes and recognised her breasts. The treachery dawned on him. In a rage he tore out the pictures, and poured red paint over Basu Lal's clean dhotis and kurtas which Gurumukh had left on the sideboard. Exhausted, he ran to the *bersati* and fell over the charpoy. Ana's voice came back to him, perspiration rose on his neck and arms, steam and smoke rose from the garden, heat and moisture pressed against his skin. He cursed and threw a stone at the Mahajans' house, mad with jealousy. Mithun ran from the house.

"What happened to Ana? Amrit, confess!" Mithun shrieked.

"I don't know!"

"Basu Lal's taken her somewhere."

"Basu Lal?"

"Yes, that old fraud. We have to go to the Taj Palace, they're having a fashion fitting."

As Amrit and Mithun pulled Mithun's bike into the Taj Palace, they saw Basu Lal pacing furiously in front of the door, to the evident amusement of the four *chowkidars.*

"Where is Ana?"

"She was supposed to meet us at the Taj for a photo shoot."

"She's gone to Bombay. With those movie people."

"You're lying."

"I saw her get into a taxi with them."

"You did this to her! You laid a trap for her! She did to it get back at you, because you . . . you . . . have no right, no . . ."

Amrit lunged at Basu Lal, who collapsed shrieking over the sidewalk. Mithun ran inside, while the security guards pulled Amrit off Basu Lal, who began to cry when he saw the tear in his silk kurta. When he got home, Amrit bribed Gurumukh to collect all of Basu Lal's drawings and clothes from the Mahajans, which Amrit then burned in the nullah. He sold his stereo system and CD collection and took a train to Bombay. To find Ana. Basu Lal called his cousin-brother, a Calcutta lawyer, and asked him to serve Mrs Mahajan with a suit for damage to his personal effects.

When Mrs Mehta opened *Stardust* to a photograph of Ana with Zafir, who hailed her as his new discovery, she promptly fainted.

Masterji

SHE WAS HERE AGAIN, IN A DIRTY HILL STATION, wasting the afternoon in a cheap restaurant, competing with a gang of Germans for the waiter's attention. Some things had improved: there was bottled water now, and the stereo was playing Bach, strangely enough, but it was still dank and freezing, the streets were glutted with plastic bags, beggars, pigs and old dogs. One could feel weariness and depletion in the air and in the soil. The waiter passed her for the fifth time. Lucy cursed, sucked deeply on her cigarette and wondered why she always came back to India.

Years before, she had come to India to defy her first husband who hated India and everything it represented: heat, vegetarians, mythology. There had been a second husband, briefly, and a third husband who insisted they stop in India on the way to Thailand, Nepal or Bali so he could visit the funeral ghats in Benaras, which she despised. This time, she believed, would be different, so it didn't matter that the hill station was squalid, the people were dull and she was bored and sick, because she was going to study with Masterji.

Masterji was recognised as a spirtual teacher in his childhood. He was educated to be a swami, but relinquished the swami's robes as a young man, graduated from Oxford with a triple first in philosophy, moved to Paris and lived with a Dutch woman who eventually became his personal secretary. He was a visiting scholar at several universities, his books had been translated into seventeen languages, his lectures always sold out, yet he lived very simply. He charged a modest fee for lecturing and put the money he earned into orphanages and health clinics in India. He usually dressed in a plain black suit and tie, he did not allow anyone to touch his feet or lie prostrate in his presence, he did not want to be regarded as a guru or a healer, but simply as a teacher.

Lucy collected gurus like furniture. Two Japanese clerics stayed in her Chelsea town house for a year. When they refused to leave she screamed and threw their suitcases out the front door. Her friend Victor said it was bad karma to raise one's voice at a holy man, to which she retorted, 'Holy men aren't freeloading layabouts,' and didn't return Victor's calls for several weeks. One morning Victor appeared at Lucy's door with a sheath of pamphlets about Masterji and took her to Masterji's lecture at the London Theosophical Society. Lucy and Victor sat in the front row. Masterji sat in an armchair on the dais beside an empty chair draped in gold silk and a spray of flowers on a side table which honoured his departed teachers. He wore a dark suit, white shirt, red tie and yellow handkerchief in his breast pocket. He had a wonderful face, a high forehead rising into a crest of white hair and beautiful, clear, intelligent eyes; his voice was so mellifluous, so assuring—perfect Oxonian inflections mingled with the subtle lilts of an Indian accent—and his ideas were so sensible; he was a remarkable combination of wisdom, strength and purity, coalesced into the person of a gracious gentleman.

When the lecture was over Lucy raced backstage to meet Masterji. Getting backstage was difficult, everyone in the auditorium wanted to meet Masterji too, but Victor knew the key people and soon they were ushered into a crowded dressing room where Masterji sat on a couch, smoking a cigarette and shaking hands. Lucy pushed her way to the front, seized Masterji's hands and insisted on giving him dinner at her town house. He declined but asked her if she would like to come to India for a private teaching he was giving in February. He did not invite Victor; Lucy noticed that Victor perspired and glared, but she didn't care, she said Absolutely, she'd go to India in February.

Lucy flew to Delhi and took an overnight train to Haridwar, the holy town where the Ganges river left the Himalayas and entered the plains. A man approached her at the railway station, dressed like one of the Kashmiri porters in a woollen vest, *salwar* and hat. He extended a hand and introduced himself as Mr Prem Joshi, the manager of Masterji's school. Prem loaded Lucy's bags into his jeep and drove her into town. She glimpsed ashrams and temples rising in pink and yellow columns above the tree line and asked if they could go to the river. She winced at the stench that rose from the nullah and was assaulted by several starving beggars who had no shoes or hats, and yet, once she descended the marble steps that led to the ghats, she was overcome by a wonderful, inexplicable mixture of calmness and fervency, anticipation and serenity that always permeated her heart and mind when she entered the Himalayas.

There were many pilgrims hanging onto chains and leaping into the freezing current, which inspired Prem to remove everything but his underwear and do three full immersions at Halki Pauri, the most auspicious of the many auspicious bathing sites. Lucy stood at the top of the steps. She lacked the courage to go into the water, though she yearned to be purged of the myriad pains accumulated over so many years of disappointments, disillusionments and failures, which she prayed would dissolve, finally, at Masterji's touch.

Lucy noticed, upon signing the register at the Himalaya Guest House that she wasn't the only person Masterji had invited to the teachings: there was an American couple, George and Serena; an elderly Swiss couple, the Rolfs; Sanjal and Dipali, two sisters from a royal family in Central India; another American girl called Sam and of all coincidences, Alicia, whom Lucy knew from New York. Many more had come for the general teachings Masterji held at the Devigunj Civic Center—most were the usual backpackers who loitered in and out of the tea stalls, leaving trails of dirt and odour. They looked so clumsy in saris, parkas and hiking boots. How could Masterji spend even five minutes on them? If they didn't know how to use a hairbrush how could they be expected to use a mantra, for God's sake?

Prem asked everyone to come to the teachings in their best clothes to show proper respect to Masterji. Lucy had a fur coat, but Prem suggested that Masterji wouldn't approve, which annoyed her. Fortunately she had several sweater sets, she refused to submit to baggy hiking pants, even though it was February and they were in the Himalayas and the servant jeered when she asked for a hot bath.

Ramesh had started working at the Himalaya Guest House when he was twelve. Shanti was fourteen and Ramesh was sixteen when they married. The furthest they had ever travelled was a pilgrimage to Gangotri, the source of the Ganges, otherwise they rarely left Devigunj. Once a month they had a Sunday off and were able to go to Haridwar to bathe and make offerings. They had prayed for a son, but since a son never came, they now prayed for good husbands for their six daughters. Prem Joshi was teaching the girls to read, which worried Shanti; she didn't want her daughters going to Dehradhun or Delhi to look for a better job. Ramesh's three brothers had servant jobs in Delhi. They visited Devigunj for only one week each year, thus, it was very hard on their wives and children. Shanti's sister's husband got a job as a driver at the American Embassy and cajoled his employer's wife into taking him to America, but after he reached New York he never wrote or sent money, not even a postcard. His family moved into a hut behind Ramesh and Shanti—the youngest girl died of tuberculosis and one of the boys ran away. Ramesh and Shanti helped as much as they could, but there was never enough money for clothes and boots and medicines for everyone, and there was never anything left to put aside for the girls' dowries. Once a year, Mrs Khanna gave the family a few old sweaters and shirts, and Prem brought clothes and blankets from his relatives in Delhi.

Ramesh always wondered if he should've tried to find work in Delhi where salaries were higher, but he liked to be in his home, to be with his own people and to speak his native dialect. He saw enough of foreigners who came for Masterji to have an idea of what Delhi was like.

Sam walked to the Shiva temple above the orchard, handed ten rupees and an orange to the widow who lived nearby, untied her boots and knelt by the *lingam* to watch the cistern drop beads of water over the stone. She opened her watercolours, but had no will to paint. Instead, she studied her hands which looked so old, the fingernails were ragged, the knuckles distended. It was depressing to be so disorganised, to be so thoroughly innured to the habits of failure and decay. She willfully neglected herself, she didn't wash her face at night the way her mother always did, she slouched, she cut her hair with sewing scissors. The only attractive thing she wore was the lapis lazuli necklace she'd bought in Manali years ago. She unhooked the clasp and dangled the necklace over her forearm. She wondered why it had once seemed so important to own it, it was just a string holding a few blue stones. She'd give the necklace to Shanti, who couldn't afford to buy jewellery.

She remembered how the valley had looked in her childhood, all brilliant magenta blossoms and viridian pine. Now the rhododendron bushes were cut down to mere stumps, the earth was picked dry—every twig, every branch was used for fuel and fodder. The mountains were being stripped bare and soon there would be nothing left to burn. She saw a shepherd woman climbing a tree to cut the higher branches to get food for her goats. All those people in the guest house had stoves filled with wood, heavy woollen blankets, electric lights, hot water for their baths—hauled from the well on Shanti's backyard and heated with wood that ought to have been used to make dinner for a hill woman's family, yet they never ceased complaining about the cold and the moisture and the inadequate faucets.

Sam pounded her fists, but it was their fault. They were just ignorant tourists; it was the timber merchants and the middle-men who built dams with foreign aid that left thousands destitute so the urban middle class could have refrigerators and televisions, like Americans. If India had followed Gandhiji, then that poor woman climbing the tree wouldn't have to worry about her sick, hungry children. An emaciated mongoose ran under a bush. There were no bears anymore, or deer. Sam fished a peanut-butter sandwich from her knapsack, left it under the bush for the mongoose, and walked back to the guest house.

Sam suffered from the curse of a brilliant childhood. She was born in Mussoorie, where her parents worked in a mission. She grew up in Benaras, Calcutta and Delhi. She spoke fluent Hindi and Bengali, she was an excellent painter and musician, in school she won several prizes for fiction and journalism. When she was eighteen she went to a university in New England where she had a protracted nervous breakdown, dropped out and fled back to India. She tried to enroll in Delhi University but eventually succumbed to her parents' demands and returned to America.

During her final year of college her father died and her mother moved to California, which left her without a home-base in India. She moved back to Delhi and spent several years in a small flat in Nizamuddin. She taught English in the Nizamuddin *busti*, freelanced as a tour guide and travel consultant and sold some of her watercolours. None of these jobs lasted or earned much money. She tried living in America again but was so miserable she returned to India.

Sam refused to sit in the dining room with the other foreigners. She ate on the kitchen floor, smoked *bidis* and played cards with the servants. She wanted to stay in the servants quarters but Mrs Khanna, the manager, would not allow an American visitor to sleep with the staff. They argued, and Sam started sleeping in the pantry. Masterji intervened and a compromise was achieved: Sam was given a little room at the back of the house next to the laundry. The servants' children were always on her bed, leafing through her books and trying on her clothes, which she often gave them. She was happy whenever she was sitting in the kitchen with Ramesh, but Mrs Khanna would inevitably thrust her head in to glare at Sam and tell Ramesh to get on his feet and do some work. Sam pressed her hands to her eyes and repeated the one prayer she remembered from her childhood: *Mother Mary give me strength, Mother Mary take me home... but there is no home, no home...*

From noon onwards, after his first smoke and drink, Jodi Khanna was cordial and endearing to his guests, as he affected the despairing charm of a man tormented by lost opportunities and unrealised ambitions. In truth he was deeply lazy—if he had ample food, liquor and tobacco, if he did not have a headache, he had all he really wanted out of life. In the mornings, he contemplated the circumscribed dimensions of his life and grieved. He knew he was wasted in a place like Devigunj, he belonged in Delhi, Bombay or

London. He could never quite visualise what he'd do if he moved to a city, he couldn't do something marginal like run a guest house or a restaurant because he wouldn't have the justification of caring for Masterji. The question of what he might do should he leave Devigunj occupied a lot of his time, and remained unsettled.

Jodi ended up running the guest house by default. He had planned to go into business with a cousin, but after several failures, all remaining schemes devolved into the guest house, the summer residence of a minor maharaja from Madhya Pradesh. A few vestigal royal flourishes had survived: Greek columns on the porch, two chandeliers, huge porcelain bathtubs which were never used. Jodi tried and failed to operate an orchard, and was about to sell the place when Masterji came for a weekend and decided it was the ideal place for his annual retreat. They built Masterji's cottage and an orphanage and converted the main residence into the guest house. Jodi's wife, Anu, decorated each room with Kashmiri upholstery, Tibetan carpets and miniature painting reproductions. For the last twelve years the rooms had always been full, Jodi had never had to worry about money.

Anu had the same complacent view of marriage as Jodi's sisters and cousins, who did not think it was necessary to keep the husband entertained as long as he was well fed. Anu was proud of having matriculated from Delhi and always told the guests about the Himachal Pradesh Ladies' Village-Uplift Society. When they were alone she described the sale at the Kailash Dry Goods Exchange and how the Saxenas were having trouble getting their son into Technical College and wasn't it too bad that Mrs Saxena couldn't keep her house clean... After years of feigning interest Jodi sat defiantly mute through these monologues. Anu obstinately pressed on, which enraged him further. Jodi's life ran smoothly, food was always available, the servants were severely disciplined; this is what Jodi expected, but lately he had come to realise that it bothered him. He could not discern when or how this shift in tolerance had occured. He suspected it was due in part to the new breed of female visitors who came to study with Masterji. The Indian women were familiar, princesses and wealthy widows, it was these foreign women who were either divorced or perpertually single, who wore pants and had peculiar hair cuts, who wanted enlightenment and sex. Jodi had resigned himself to conjugal terms dictated by Anu, wherein sex was periodically granted if she wanted a visit from her mother or a trip to Delhi. Anu had produced two children, a son and daughter, both in a nearby boarding school, which, in Anu's opinion, was unimpeachable proof of her fulfilment of all past and future marital duties.

But Jodi brimmed with sexual ambition. He was handsome, though his stomach was getting somewhat too large. One night Jodi tried his luck on a dim, pale New Zealander. Anu had gone to Delhi, Jodi invited the woman to dinner, plied her with scotch and listened to the tales of woe that had catalysed her spiritual quest. He attempted a kiss, at which point she hurled herself into his lap. He enjoyed the furtive messiness of it, but the following morning she declared undying love. For the next few months he did nothing more than drink scotch and speculate about what kind of underwear lurked under which jeans and parka.

Eventually, Jodi tried and succeeded on an American and a Swiss, and thus emboldened, he attempted to cull a liaison from each crop of visitors. He didn't like the way the foreign women looked. Of the current group Alicia was the most attractive, though too tall and thin. Serena was pallid, Lucy was too old and peculiar. Sanjal and Dipali had full breasts and hips, long hair and amber skin. They were cleansed and tended by legions of family servants. They spread noise and chaos, they were accustomed to having huge palaces to wreck and huge staffs to clean up. Dipali, married with two small children assigned to a passive nursemaid, carried herself with the demure lethargy he expected of an Indian woman, whereas Sanjal, unmarried and childless, smoked cigarettes and drank whiskey and wore tight velvet pants and leather boots with perilously high heels. Jodi wondered how many men she'd been to bed with. Quite a few, he suspected. She had that look about her, restless and dissatified, hungry for food and liquor and attention. When she leaned back he could see her breasts pushing against her silk shirt and her velvet pants tight around her hips. She didn't seem to mind his eyes running back and forth across her torso, she seemed accustomed to attention. He wondered how to go about it, it would be difficult because she wouldn't let him forget that she was a royal, which infuriated and aroused him.

"I wish Alicia would just snap out of it and marry this nice fellow who's madly in love with her. I know he's dull, but he has money, not as much as hers, but enough to walk out on her if it comes to that." Lucy pulled a brush through her brass-coloured hair, which was darker and brassier than Serena remembered it to be when they had met at Masterji's lecture in Paris. Lucy was wearing a white cashmere sweater over a silk blouse, white flannel trousers, an embroidered gold and white shawl. She was unquestionably the best-dressed woman in Himachal Pradesh. Her body was small, but she had a collosal presence, ruled by her huge, ferocious eyes. She bore them like a curse, as if for those two flaws of beauty she was destined to have weak husbands.

"You know, of course, that Alicia is very strange."

"She seems normal to me." Serena's attention drifted to an Italian fashion magazine on the side-table.

"I promise you, she isn't. It's that crazy childhood. I had one too but at least I had plenty of cousins to play with. All she had was one much, much older half-sister and an awful nanny. Her father is an unreformed playboy, he's always gotten away with it because he's fabulously handsome, and her mother's not the nicest person you ever met. The mother walked in on him with her sister, she tried to kill him, and the story goes that Alicia had to take the knife out of her hand. I first met her when she was about thirteen. The most beautiful little girl's face with the manners of a thirty-five old banker! I must warn you, she's tight as a thimble."

"As a what?"

"If the bill is fifty cents she'll ask you for your twenty-five. Money does awful things to people. Is George mad at me?"

"No . . ."

"Then why did he ignore me at dinner?"

"He wasn't ignoring you."

"I thought he was."

"He's just preoccupied."

"Alright, I believe you. Now tell me, how do I look?" Lucy leaned before the mirror and rearranged her necklaces and the awning of gold hair above her brow.

"You look wonderful." She looked alright, Serena decided, How old was she? She had to be in her early fifties, it was a shame her distended eyes made her so unattractive and made her behave like a large, frustrated child, always afraid of being left out.

"Sometimes Masterji acts like he doesn't know who I am. He picked me out of all those people in London and now I think he's forgotten who I am."

"Isn't that just his way?"

"He doesn't treat George like that. Or that Sam girl."

"Why don't you talk to him about it?"

"Talk about it! Heavens, I can't do that."

"Why not?"

"Because I'd be much too embarrassed to bring it up. I mean, what if it's true?" Lucy opened a jar of Serena's cold cream and dotted the white gel over her cheeks. "Thank God I never went in for sunbathing. I've got thirty percent fewer wrinkles than all my friends who roasted through their twenties and thirties." She patted the gel into her skin and touched her mouth with an orange lipstick. "So when are you having your private audience with Masterji? Don't you want one?"

"Not really."

"Why not?"

"Because I don't have anything to say to him."

"Serena, you ought to hear yourself. George can get one for you like that. I put in my request for a private audience the moment I stepped out of the taxi and I'm still waiting for the nod. Imagine being all alone with him, having those divine dark eyes looking right into you!" Lucy hugged her breasts. "And do you know he sometimes gives you this *kundalini* thing when you're doused in this amazing white light and all you feel is perfect, total bliss! I don't understand you, here you are practically married to Masterji's favourite person and you spend the whole day in your room reading novels. Life's simply not fair." Lucy rummaged through Serena's drawers. "Oh that reminds me, I've got to give my laundry while there's an ounce of sunlight." Lucy ran out, leaving Serena's drawers open.

Serena pulled her quilt over her head. She didn't want audiences or blessings, she wanted to marry George. In the beginning they had postponed marriage so he could finish his master's degree in comparative religion. Then two years ago George heard Masterji speak at the YMCA and announced to her that he had just had the most important meeting of his life. George joined Masterji at a French chateau for a seven-month retreat, Serena dutifully followed.

The chateau was a damp, gloomy barn filled with Masterji's other students, most of whom had taken vows of silence. Serena hated it but when they arrived in Devigunj, Serena was briefly nostalgic about the chateau, where she had French food and the *Herald Tribune.* The Himalayan Guest House had no central heating, no hot water, a library composed of books on Hindu philosophy and spy novels, the town was decrepit with a few dirty tea stalls.

Serena couldn't discern any fault with Masterji. He did not stay in expensive hotels, he wore simple clothes, he treated waiters, reporters, movie stars and politicians with the same gracious equanimity. His only vice was cigarettes, filterless French cigarettes. It wasn't Masterji that bothered her, it was the way George had changed under Masterji's influence. He began to meditate three hours a day and to recite special prayers six times a day. He talked endlessly about getting out of the cycle of rebirth, understanding the nature of impermanence, practising detachment, surrendering to the guru who would deliver them from *samsara.*

Serena kept waiting to feel something in her head or heart when Masterji spoke—everyone else gazed in awe, some cried and shook and fell on the floor. But Masterji sounded like just another well-read, middle-aged Indian man with an English accent. George interpreted every word out of Masterji's mouth as a sacred command. When Masterji said that messy rooms weakened the aura by creating an etheric pattern of decay, George spent three hours reorganising the luggage, refolding all the clothes, putting caps on shampoo and cologne bottles. At the next teaching, Masterji said it was important to respect the written word. That night George took all the printed matter available (including a five-year-old *Woman's Day* and two dress catalogues) out of the wastebasket, dusted them, put them on the altar and laid a rose over them. He then started taking cold showers because hot water killed microbes. Serena was furious, all of these so-called "spiritual" rules interfered with life as intelligently and realistically lived.

To avoid Lucy's inquisitions and Anu's invitations, Alicia often walked to Devigunj and had tea in the bazaar or wandered in the back lanes with buffaloes and pigs and bad sewage. She lingered in the gullies; she inhaled all the vapours, even those that burned and hurt; she watched women sorting grain, old men pushing bicycles loaded with milk, cows resting in patches of sunlight. Devigunj had a mosque, an old Anglican church, a small Sikh gurudwara and many Hindu temples. Most of the temples were filthy; the worshippers pushed and cursed and stole money out of each other's shirts, the new temples were swathed with blinking lights and played *bhajans* at piercing volume, yet every time Alicia saw a temple her hands joined at her heart, she joined the line of worshippers buying puja baskets with marigold garlands, sugar and candlewicks and handed them to the priests. Sometimes she felt a peculiar urge to kneel in front of the idols, but she was afraid of what people might think. Everywhere she saw deities, of every form and colour: their eyes sparkled back at her from *bidi* wrappers, tree trunks, taxi windows. Instinctively, she saluted them, even if she didn't know their names or what they stood for.

Don Williams, the American movie star, arrived on the first day of the teachings to a shooting schedule in Los Angeles. The students assembled in Masterji's private cottage above the apple orchard. Chairs and cushions were arranged in a semicircle around Masterji's armchair. Masterji put a fresh bowl of flowers before the empty chair draped with a saffron silk cloth and sat in his blue velvet armchair with his legs crossed, a white shawl draped over his knees and shoulders, smoking his filterless French cigarettes.

The room was cold; Masterji didn't want to have a fire except at night because wood was so scarce and he didn't want to live far better than the farmers and shepherds who inhabited small huts along the hillside. When all the students were seated Masterji rubbed his hands, shook out his feet and slowly peered around the room, taking full measure of the pictures on the walls, the rain dripping against the window, the curls of incense smoke rising from the ashtray at his feet. He cleared his throat, looked down into his lap and began to speak.

"I am sure that each of you has wondered why I've asked you to come to these teachings. I didn't want to tell you before because I wanted to see if you would come regardless of my specific purpose. I have several small groups of students from all parts of the world. From each group I am going to select someone to be initiated as one of my chief disciples, to carry on my work. I've just been diagnosed as having lung cancer. I'm sure that I'll die soon. I'm not worried about it, for as we have incarnated again and again, we have also died again and again. My work now is to pass on the lineage of these into the next century, especially in the West. I will see who is marked for the task. Certain signs will come to me in dreams, conversations and intuitions. The one among you who is ready for this initiation will come forward of her or his own accord. At the time the chief disciple is chosen, a clear path and purpose will become apparent to each of you. We are all blessed to share in this discovery. We shall all be linked by it, and we shall all incarnate together in the future. I do not expect my initiates to lead an ascetic life or wear religious robes—I don't wear them, as you know. Rather I expect him or her to live in the world so as to understand how most people are living. This is the reason why we have all come together at this time. Remember, I did not choose any of you, you chose to come to me."

Masterji started coughing violently. Prem handed him a glass of water. Everyone cleared their throats and shifted on the cushions, no words were exchanged, all eyes flickered in curiosity and amazement. After swallowing his medicine and another cup of tea, Masterji continued with his regular teaching about compassion and service.

Lucy drummed her pencil against her notebook. Would Masterji be watching every little thing to see who was holier and better? She'd better get rid of her fur coat once and for all. George sat erect, his eyes glowing with rapture. Clearly it had to be George, he was the most devoted of the lot, so attentive and reliable. But poor Serena, he wasn't making her happy in the least, that was a point against him. And what of Alicia, with all that money and education and the additional bonus of good looks? But she was a little too perfect, so perfect she was sort of ordinary really, not good for a disciple. The Rolfs were the wild cards, one doubted if they understood a single word of Masterji, yet every morning, there they were in the breakfast room, downing hot milk and reading their religious booklets, and they were always the first to arrive at the teachings, with sharpened pencils, wearing their matching sweater sets. Who knew what went on in those tidy little Swiss brains of theirs? They never gossiped or made a mess but they were always after the cook to reheat the vegetables and pay more attention to the amount of salt he used. So may be it would be the Rolfs, but what then of Rani Dipali and her sister Sanjal? The Rani wasn't much of a conversationalist, her sister was the more intriguing of the two, but they didn't seem too terribly interested in meditation, they were clearly just on holiday.

Prem was the perfect Indian disciple: devoted, quiet, not bad looking either, but he was already employed as Masterji's secretary, so he was out. Don Williams? No, no, that would be just too obvious. That odd woman Sam was American, and Masterji did say that the initiate would be a Western leader (then what were the Rani, Sanjal and Prem doing here?). But he couldn't pick that sorry little waif in her poncho and felt hat.

Lucy had gone through the whole group, which left only herself. Her brain oscillated, it was entirely possible, she had as much of a chance as anyone else. Masterji had asked her, not Victor, that day in London. And she had all the connections and houses that were just perfect for spiritual meetings. Maybe it would be her... she had always been ignored—by her family, by people she'd wanted to work with. Could it be that this was it? For an instant she saw herself as the one, she saw thousands of faces gazing up at her from rows and rows of huge auditoriums, she saw ex-husbands, ex-friends, cousins and siblings, chastened and envious for having misused and lost her, and she saw Masterji, beaming wisdom and serenity at her side.

After the teachings, the Rolfs went straight to their rooms, beat the rugs, shook the cushions, dusted all the furniture, scrubbed the floor and polished their framed pictures of Masterji, Sai Baba, Ramakrishna and Chidvilasananda. Mrs Khanna shouted for Ramesh and Shanti, but they had gone to the market at her instructions. Anu went up to the Rolfs' room to apologise for her errant staff, but the Rolfs told her that they were fully responsible for purifying their own environment and wanted to continue doing it by themselves. They also asked permission to wash their own dishes after meals.

"Guess what I just heard?" Lucy exclaimed, storming into Serena's room. "The Rolfs got a private audience with Masterji! I can't believe it."

"Why not?" Serena hoisted herself on an elbow, just high enough to glimpse at herself in the mirror.

"They're the first to get one! I've been asking since I arrived and still that Prem tells me it may be tomorrow when Masterji's health improves. It's just the worst kind of favouritism." Lucy pulled a cigarette from her bag and snapped the lid of an engraved silver lighter.

"I didn't know you smoked?"

"I am now. I've been trying to be so utterly perfect, I've stopped wearing furs, eating meat, the works. I've got to talk to Masterji, I'm having a crisis, for Godsakes, doesn't anyone care?"

"What's wrong?"

"Oh, the usual horror, I have to decided when and how to divorce my husband."

"Are you still in love with him?"

"That's hardly the point, I can't remember when or if we were ever in love, let's say that sorting out our assets is complicated. It will take at least a year to divide all the furniture and paintings and decide who gets which house. I've seen all my friends get tied up in knots trying to keep everything when the divorce comes, so it's easier just to let Damion take what he wants, but what galls me is that he bought it all with my money. It isn't good to be married to a man who acts like a mistress." Lucy inhaled her cigarette and pressed copper fingernails into her elbows. "I'm sure they've got a plan to get the initiation. Everyone does, except you, of course, you don't care. Or Alicia. She doesn't take the teachings seriously at all."

"But I always see her reading Masterji's books in the library."

"She's just pretending. She's always pretended to be a good little girl because obedience is the first line of self-defense. I'll bet you anything she gets an audience before I do. It's the long hair and the legs, that's where money pays off, all that riding and swimming in the summers. Masterji's a man like all the rest, they always melt before the high altar of the tall, slim and rich. I don't see that she's really that exceptional looking."

"She's cold." In Serena's view all attractive women were rivals until proven inferiors.

"That's what the men love. She's fully aware of her power over men while she pretends to be ignorant." Lucy crushed her cigarette into the heel of her boot. "I've got to think of something that will show Masterji I'm serious about everything he says."

"Why don't you talk to George?"

"George isn't going to give away any secrets."

"What secrets?"

"Oh, never mind!" Lucy heard Don William's voice in the hallway and ran after it.

Masterji continued with his afternoon lectures, oblivious to the wind and hail pounding against the windows. One night the wind broke down his door, he caught a chill and cancelled teachings for three days. The weather made it impossible to take a walk or go to the bazaar for tea or shopping. Ramesh, Shanti, Amla and their other daughters were exhausted by demands for tea, toast, hot water, clean clothes; the laundry took three days to dry, hanging on the clothes-line in the servants' rooms; bath water had to be carried on the servants' backs through mud and rain.

Every Friday, Prem took an offering to the Chamunda temple in memory of his mother. In the rain it took him over an hour to walk down the hill and back. When he arrived back at the guest house, Shanti brought him hot milk and a dry blanket. Sanjal, George, Serena and Dipali were playing Monopoly in the dining room, Alicia sat on the couch, reading.

"Here comes our little pilgrim!" Sanjal smiled. "You've purified yourself while George has just snatched Park Place from under my nose." Sanjal yawned and stretched her arms, exposing a trunk of taut golden flesh between bands of magenta silk. She was like a rich desert left out in the sun, the black *kajal* around her eyes melted into her skin, which melted into her silk clothes and hair that seeped over the couch and cushions

"I can't believe you went out in this weather." Serena pushed her hands into her sublimely warm, fur-lined leather gloves which George forbade her to wear around Masterji.

"I don't mind, it's a small gesture, for all my mother did for me in her lifetime."

"I like bad weather," said George. "It makes it easier to study."

"Masterji often praises your discipline."

"It's hardly discipline. I find it enormously pleasurable."

Prem signalled a *namaste* to Shanti as she dropped four cubes of sugar into his tea. He was, Alicia observed, remarkably handsome. His face had an exquisite line and expression with the most sensuous hair, skin and eyebrows. She admired his fingers as they reached for his teacup and spoon—she always paid careful attention to men's hands.

"How long have you worked with Masterji?"

"About ten years. I met him when he came to lecture at Oxford. I wanted to return to India to do social work, but I didn't want to be with a big development agency. I discussed it with Masterji and he asked me to run the school and the orphanage."

"His health is getting worse, isn't it?" asked George.

"Yes, unfortunately. He isn't as worried about it as we are. We're very lucky to spend this time him. While he's still got some strength, he's putting all his effort into the transmission of the teachings and the *shaktipat*."

Serena squinted at Prem. "What's that?"

"The *shaktipat*? The *shakti*, which lies dormant at the base of the spine, rises through the seven *chakras* to the crown of the head. For many people it is the turning point out of *samsara*. It happens through sight or touch of a master. Some people experience it upon seeing Masterji walk across a room. For others it happens when he touches the forehead."

"Is that the sign that he's chosen you for the initiation?"

"No, it can happen at any time, to anyone. It's a blessing, it means that you'll be linked to the guru in future lifetimes as you successively purify your karma and move towards the final liberation. For some people it doesn't happen at all, no matter how much time they spend with Masterji."

"I couldn't endure any future lifetimes," Sanjal yawned. "I can't imagine going through all this tediousness again, especially school."

George tucked his money and property deeds under the Monopoly board. "Speaking of which, I've got to start my afternoon prayers."

"And leave our Monopoly game like so much unfinished business?" cried Sanjal. "Only now have I got some Free Parking."

Alicia locked herself in her room and pretended to be ill so she wouldn't have to go to Anu's dinner. She felt a constricting, sickening loneliness, mixed with self-disgust, as she realised that she wasn't having a good time because she was dependent on servants, central heating, hot water. She lay in the dark, cataloguing incidents that confirmed her self-loathing. She remembered sending her poetry to a publisher who dismissed it as indulgent tripe. They sat in a shiny atrium, deafened by an enormous fountain, she remained stoically poised as he insulted her ideas, she hid the poems in the back of a drawer and later burned them. She was crushed, she had genuinely believed that they were good, it reinforced her mother's insistence that she had neither talent nor luck.

She realised why she didn't like Don Williams, he resembled someone she had, in a moment of weakness and sloth, allowed to seduce her. She winced and pressed her face into the mattress, to remember the man's mouth and eyebrows, his hands around her waist. It was so humiliating to know a mistake, when in the midst of making it. Of course, one always stumbled into mistakes on the pretense of fulfilling life's promise of romantic adventure, which still drove her onto airplanes, into trysts, made her squander money to impress people or drive them away. She felt time both encroaching and retreating; she felt the oppressive weight of unfulfilled expectations; she wondered why most of her life had devolved into vague, inconsistent recollections, that added up to so little.

Alicia, Dipali and Sanjal heard that Prem was driving to Haridwar and asked for a ride. The storm had thrown so many trees and boulders on the road that they didn't reach Haridwar until late afternoon. Prem went into a stationary store, Alicia followed Dipali and Sanjal to a shop called Varma Styles and Suiting. Mr Varma, dozing by the cash box, bolted to attention when he heard Sanjal's voice. He pinned the three women against the wall with tea and sodas as bolts of cloth were unfurled, embroidery and beading came out of drawers and off shelves, while he pleaded with Sanjal and Dipali to take note of the beautiful work and the excellent quality. He was also eager to tell his life story: his family had fled Lahore during partition and he had rebuilt his life, first in Lucknow and then in Haridwar, but now his wife was going deaf and his only son had died of heart failure. The boy's picture hung behind hung framed in silver with a string of fresh roses around it. Alicia offered some consolation but Sanjal and Dipali paid no attention whatsoever. They pulled the fabric to test the weave, they complained that the blues were dull and asked to see the reds, they scowled at the prices and threatened to leave. Mr Varma shouted in defence, Sanjal waved her hands in disgust and stood up. Mr Varma flung a heap of silk at her feet.

Dipali picked it up and tossed it back. Mr Varma howled like a wounded animal.

Finally, Sanjal pointed to a piece of orange poplin and dropped a handful of rupees at Mr Varma's feet. She complained of thirst. Mr Varma sent one boy to fetch a cold soda while another fanned her with an old newspaper. They sat for another fifteen minutes while Dipali, Sanjal and Mr Varma discussed the price of silver and the difficulty of finding a good tailor. When Sanjal stood started to leave Mr Varma insisted that she take just one more item. He pulled out a pile of saris, Dipali fingered the borders and asked to see the blouse-pieces. They passed them back and forth: Sanjal bought three blouse-pieces and a petticoat, Dipali bought a piece of red silk.

Sanjal and Dipali wandered towards the silversmith who already had tea and sodas waiting. They studied a tray of toe rings and anklets and began removing shoes and socks to try them on. Alicia trailed behind, then went to the bathing ghats. The evening sky was red, the air smelled of tobacco, cooking oil, overripe fruit. Alicia heard the ring of temple chimes mixed with a film song from a radio. A group of trekkies argued with a taxi driver. No one but Lucy called them hippies. They were more organised than the hippies: they had hepatitis shots, mosquito nets and waterproof luggage, though they still followed the old hippie migration routes—winter in Goa, summer in Nepal, with stops in Benaras, Pushkar and Rishikesh. A few spectral reminders of the hippie era floated about the edges of the bazaar in faded satin pants and dreadlocks, smoking chillums, eating in filthy *dhabas*, drinking tap water, almost as a point of honour. Alicia paused at a book stall, someone tapped her shoulder.

"Hi, I'm Rami. I'm sorry to impose on you but I haven't eaten for three days and I don't have any money." He was a young American in a dirty saffron robe, his head was shaved and his ears and nose were pierced with bits of tin, he had wide cheeks, gentle eyes with dark lashes.

"Could we have a cup of tea together, in there?" He pointed to the Gupta Beverage and Snack House.

Alicia was instinctively suspicious of anyone who asked her for money, especially a man, but his mixture of boldness and helplessness reminded her of her stepbrother Tony who had come to India years ago and was found dead in the Bombay railway station. But the stranger seemed genuinely lonely, he was obviously destitute, so she nodded and followed him into the Gupta Beverage and Snack House. They ordered tea, *samosas* and cheese sandwiches. Rami ate ravenously and ordered seconds.

"How long have you been in India?" Alicia asked.

"Four years—no—sorry, five years. I've been a sadhu for four years. My first year I was just hanging out." He glanced up between bites with an affable, wholly American smile.

"Why did you become a sadhu?"

He wiped his mouth on his robe and shrugged. "I don't really know, it just happened. I went to Poona and I was looking for this hotel when a man came up to me in the street, gave me this robe and started touching my feet and calling me Ramji. So I gave away everything I had, shaved my head and went barefoot."

"Why?"

"I don't know. It was, like, my penance, it just felt right to do it. So I walked everywhere, I never took a taxi or a bus, if I felt really sick or something, maybe I'd take a rickshaw. I walked to Calcutta, Gangotri, Rameshwaram and back again. I begged outside temples and slept on the ground. Once I got really sick and a sweeper family took me in for a month, I guess it's good karma to take care of sadhus." He squinted and rubbed blunt, ragged fingers across his forehead. "Now I want to go back to California and see my mother but I don't have enough money for a plane ticket. Can I have another soda?" Alicia nodded, Rami went into the kitchen. His feet were hugely swollen and covered with running sores. He came back with a Limca and emptied his bag on the table. "I'm selling some stuff to get money for my plane ticket." He had a watch, a pewter bangle, some hashish, two bead necklaces. Alicia fingered a necklace to avoid his eyes, she could feel them bearing down on her in desperation. India was full of people who were born wretchedly poor, this man had willingly embraced poverty and now he was asking her to relieve him of it. But she could see that he was frightened, that he was fleeing death, in the same way that Tony had devoured drugs and money and strangers and then pleaded to be rescued. She dropped some crumpled rupees on the table, he grabbed the notes and counted them.

"What d'you want, the necklace?"

"No, no, just keep it."

"Can you get more?"

"I, I don't know... if you want another sandwich, go ahead." She saw more running sores on his chest and arms. Suddenly she wanted to get away from him. He went back to the kitchen, she ran out of the door, through the bazaar, down to the ghats, terrified that he was following her. She tripped on a rock and fell down a flight of steps. She tried to stand but her ankle collapsed in pain. A beggar girl crawled over, grasped her foot and worked her thumbs over the sprain. The girl's legs were shrivelled and deformed but her face and arms were beautiful, as if two bodies had been attached by mistake. The girl held out a tin plate with a crude idol draped with wilted marigolds and asked for baksheesh. Alicia searched her pockets, but they were empty, and she was annoyed that she'd given her money to a dharma bum in a tea shop and had nothing for the girl. She looked at her hands and saw a gold ring, a gift from her mother. She slipped it off and pressed it into the girl's palm. Alarmed, the girl pushed the ring into her blouse and limped swiftly up the stairs. Alicia knew her mother would be angry, she never dispensed any jewellery without an accompanying lecture about heirlooms and personal responsibility. Alicia would have to remember to tell her the ring was left in a hotel bathroom, which her mother would consider less tragic than the idea of squandering gold on a beggar.

Alicia descended the ghats to the edge of the water. Light splintered over the Ganges, monkeys and vultures picked at rotting garbage, a line of beggars held out shrivelled hands and stumps that were once hands. She was surrounded by stench and filth and crippled bodies but the river looked so pure and the air was so clear, she knelt into the water and let its wonderful coolness grasp her legs and hands. It was strange . . . all she felt was beauty, serenity and perfection.

That night Alicia had a dream about Rami. She awoke at dawn in a hot sweat, thinking that she should've given the rupees to the beggar girl and the gold ring to Rami to help him buy a plane ticket. Three days later she had another dream that Rami had died.

Jodi and Sanjal sat drinking scotch in the library. It was past midnight, Sanjal was fairly drunk, Jodi portioned his drinks carefully so as not to fumble whatever opportunity might arise.

"I'm telling you, Jodi*bhai*, Indian men are the worst. They belong to their mothers, totally and completely, they don't give a damn what the wife wants. All these foreigners come here to see Khajuraho, but I'm telling you, Indian sex is for rot." Sanjal's make-up was smudged, there was a wide hole in her stocking and her hair was a tangled nest, but the general effect was very attractive.

"I think you've been with the wrong fellows . . ."

"Naturally, I've only been with royals. Why do you think the maharajas lost power in India? Too many servants, whores and medicines. Wealth makes for impotence, except for the Italians and the French; in those cases only does wealth improve the thing." She poured another drink, with a groan. "But foreigners are so, argh, you know what I'm saying. No respect, they have no respect for women. The way they make their women slave in office and do all the housecleaning, no time off when the baby comes. Look at those foreign girls, so bony and frumpy." She grimaced and leaned back on the couch. Her skirt travelled further up her thighs to hover at the uppermost edge of her stockings. Despite the wanton fullness of bosom and her practiced sneer, she looked like a sad little girl. It seemed the perfect moment to strike.

"Come come, my dear, don't fret." Jodi slid an arm around her shoulder. "Beautiful women always have a difficult time of it. But you've got friends . . ."

"Friends, friends, what friends? Only parasites, flatterers, always wanting something. Only Masterji has a pure motive. Dipali offered him the use of the palace with the whole staff last year but he said No, he preferred a simple surrounding." She leapt up and paced about the room. "Jodi*bhai*, I really think I should give up everything and come here to live with Masterji."

"It's a purer way of life." Jodi furrowed his brow into what he hoped looked like sensitive concern.

"We've all grown up hearing about Ram and Sita and the Pandavas in the forest, thinking how good it is to go off and live in exile like that, to live simply with nature, no fancy dress, no car. But look at us, turning our backs on our heritage, living in a Bombay high-rise . . ." Sanjal fell on the couch, "I want to stay here in the mountains, away from everything."

"You can stay as long as you like." Jodi quickly kissed

her on the mouth, ran his hands through her hair and across her shoulders, until she pushed him away.

"Come on, not that."

"What my dear? You seem so unhappy..." He left one hand in her hair.

"I am. I'm desperately unhappy." She grabbed the whiskey and refilled her glass.

"Please tell me why?"

"I just told you why."

"Of course, but give me more details."

"Only Masterji can give guidance. I must have a real talk with him, without Dipali or anyone poking in. Can you get me a private interview?"

"That shouldn't be a problem at all."

"But it is, you don't know how the others are hogging his free time. That Lucy is pestering Prem day and night for not one but two, four, eight private audiences!"

Jodi repositioned himself near her torso. "Consider it done. Tomorrow afternoon."

"Really and truly?"

"Of course," he leaned in to kiss her again, she let him go on.

In his teachings, Masterji frequently discussed the power of thought, how mental images shaped physical reality. This troubled Serena who had created complex daydreams to escape the tedium of Devigunj and the guest house. Another daily entertainment, especially during the teachings, was evaluating the others in the group. George warned her not to project unkind thoughts, but she was sure everyone else did it, too. They all talked a lot about charity and selflessness when, in fact, only Prem worked for the orphanage. Don made stupid, violent movies filled with rapes and killings, so what was he doing here, talking about peace and global unity? Lucy and Sanjal argued and gossiped, Alicia was a snob, she got away with it because all the men thought she was so attractive. Serena had supreme faith in her own beauty—from childhood her mother and aunt and grandmother had reassured her about it. All women made harsh judgements of each other's beauty, or the lack of it; Serena reasoned these private vindications were indispensable for survival.

Three times a week Anu invited the group to dinner, which Serena found hideously boring. The guests were expected at 7.30 but the food didn't make an appearance until well past nine.

Serena tried to get out of Anu's Saturday night dinner party, but George insisted because it was Alicia and Jodi Khanna's birthdays. Don, Dipali and Sanjal managed to avoid Anu's dinners, though on account of the joint birthdays, the royal sisters had been commandeered. Don, the third royal, remained at large.

Jodi made no effort to conceal his irritation at being the centerpiece. He tapped his foot against the table, chewed loudly on peanuts, yawned and blew his nose. Anu tried to distract the guests with little jokes about Jodi's carpentry projects, Jodi responded by chewing and yawning louder.

"So Alicia, how old are you today?" Anu pulled her pink sari taut across her bosom.

"I'm twenty-eight."

"My goodness, twenty-eight! So you haven't pursued the spiritual life before now?"

"I was taught that good works were a spiritual practice. My family funds several philanthropic organisations in New York."

"I find that my work with the Ladies Himachal Rural Uplift Society is a definite invigoration." Anu placed a basket of potato chips on an embroidered doily in the center of the coffee table. "Who's there? Ah, Sam . . ." Anu forced a grin as Sam pulled a stool to Jodi's elbow and slipped him a new pack of cigarettes.

"Where'd you get those fabulous shoes?" George adjusted his glasses to study Sam's feet.

"Kathmandu." Sam's eyes flickered over Alicia's complexion, torso and pearl earrings. Girls like Alicia made Sam very uncomfortable, they had homes and credit cards and matching socks, their clothes and hair fell in perfect contours over their legs and arms, they were absolutely certain of their place in the world. Her own poverty enraged her, nothing in her childhood had prepared her for it.

"Mr Khanna, could tell us why was there a protest march in the bazaar yesterday?" asked George.

"It's about the dam that the World Bank is funding in the next valley," Sam cut in, "60,000 villagers are about to be displaced."

"But won't the dam bring electricity to the cities, which is what India needs?"

"Yes, it'll only help the middle men and the industrialists. The World Bank has displaced millions of villagers all over the world. It was the World Bank and AID that funded the road into the Amazon which allowed beef producers to bulldoze the rainforest."

"The world is quite finished." Sanjal patted her gold necklace into place.

"Sam wants everyone in India to go back to spinning and wearing *khadi*." Jodi lit one of Sam's *bidis*.

"Everyone in India would be a lot better off that way."

"That's a tiresomely sentimental attitude, my dear."

"You don't have to call me 'dear', honey."

"What a war of words!" trilled Anu. "Everyone must be getting hungry, isn't it?"

Sam glared at Jodi. "When was the last time you made your own food or washed your own clothes?"

"I've never made my own food because I'm a bad cook and my wife does my laundry because she enjoys it."

"Our special birthday dinner is served!" Anu clapped her

hands and beckoned the guests towards the serving dishes, arranged on her new handblock table runner from Fab India. Serena prayed that no one would talk to her, she was deeply immersed in a daydream about giving a dinner party in New York and the marvellous impression it would make with George's friends. George politely nodded and smiled as Anu described her brother's duties as a sub-inspector for the Haryana Development Agency. The Rolfs helped themselves to third and fourth helpings of food and promptly left. Sam went to the kitchen to eat with Shanti and Ramesh.

"Now we've got a special birthday surprise! Oh, no, the shop's made a mistake with the names." Anu presented the cake, decorated with seven candles and a plastic hummingbird for no apparent reason; it said, Happy Birthday Lucy loves Jodi.

"Thank God it isn't my real birthday, I can't bear to be reminded of how ancient I am, but I'll take all your happy returns anyway!" Lucy lunged forward and blew out all the candles. Alicia leaned over for a piece of cake, Jodi caught a glimpse of her breasts, harnessed in white lace. He speculated, but it would be too much work, negotiating through her rich-girl hauteur. She was an American model of Sanjal and Dipali, probably worse, for having read a few more books.

"What is she doing in there?" Sanjal frowned towards the kitchen where the servant's laughter mingled with Sam's Hindi.

Anu poured tea into her pink and white china cups. "She enjoys making conversation with the servants. It is a nice experience for them to meet someone from another culture."

"She shouldn't be sitting on the kitchen floor, it isn't ladylike." Dipali held her nails against her blouse to see if the colours matched. Sanjal chewed a handful of nuts and gulped half a glass of whiskey. Jodi reached for the whiskey bottle next to Sanjal's conspicuous left thigh and caught the scent of her jasmine hair oil. Dipali counted her gold bangles and yawned without bothering to cover her mouth.

Lucy dismissed Sam as another mangy hippie until she overheard her speaking fluent Hindi one afternoon. Then Lucy admired a beautiful watercolour in Jodi's dining room which, it turned out, was painted by Sam. So she had some education and talent, and Lucy deduced an attractive figure beneath Sam's pants and sweaters, though no one would ever know it from the way she slouched over the table, twirling *bidis* between her fingers, with those brooding eyes, short hair tucked into an embroidered cap. She wasn't a lesbian, Lucy was sure if it, word had it that she'd been madly in love with an Indian boy.

"She has a definite chip on her shoulder. She's mad about something, life's dealt her talent without luck. Poor thing." Lucy tested Serena' perfume. "I suppose we ought to feel sorry for her. She always eats on the kitchen floor, she's afraid to come into the dining room when we're having breakfast. She must be embarrassed, after all, we've got money, she wears those Indian sandals with woolly socks and sleeps in that closet by the laundry room. I suppose she can't afford anything better."

"Maybe we should help her. She is part of the group," said Serena.

"You mean pay for her to stay in a better room?"

"She might not feel so left out if she got to stay with us."

"What a wonderful way to get good karma all around! Masterji will absolutely love it. Alicia and I will put up the seed money. I'll go speak with her at once." Lucy heard music in Don's room and realised that she now had a good reason to go in and talk with him. The door was ajar, she knocked, he said, Come in and she did, on mincing steps. Don lay across his bed, his arms crossed behind his head.

His hair and forehead were wet, his torso gleamed with oil. Lucy felt a thrill of danger to have caught him alone and practically undressed.

"Donny, oh, may I call you Donny?"

"Sure, man." He yawned and brushed golden bangs off his brow.

"We've got a little situation developing here and I'd so love to get your advice on it. There's one member of our group who isn't in the same league money wise, you do know what I mean, and I think she feels rather badly about it. I very much want to help her out so that she feels herself on an equal footing with everyone. Isn't that what the teachings are all about?"

"Yeah, I guess."

"I thought we'd take up a collection to get her into a better room and give her some pocket money so she can really delve into the teachings and keep up with the rest of us."

"Sounds cool." Don stood up and shook out his legs and arms. Lucy took note of each carefully honed muscle pulsing beneath his blue sweat pants.

"So I wondered, I mean, I've got more cash than I know what to do with, so I'm going to put up the seed funds and then everyone else could just . . ." Lucy saw his attention drift, and changed the subject at once. "I don't know how you can go about barefoot, I'm shivering in leather boots!"

"I can get into cold." Don started doing sit-ups.

"Aren't the teachings just marvellous?"

"Pretty heavy stuff." He turned over for push-ups.

"Aren't you going mad wondering who's going to get the nod from Masterji?" Don finished his push-ups and pulled off his sweatpants, revealing miniscule black underpants. Lucy decided to pretend that nothing unusual was happening, though she was reeling to be alone with the unclothed Don

Williams. Who would've dreamed such things could happen on a spiritual retreat.

"Lucy? Oh sorry —" Serena peeked through the door.

"Come in man, we're just hanging around," Lucy fumed. Wasn't it clear she and Don were having a private moment?

"I've spoken with the Rolfs and they've contributed this for Sam." Serena handed Lucy an envelope.

"Good, thanks." Lucy hid the envelope under her arm and signalled Serena to leave the room.

"Are you okay?"

"Yes, thanks again . . ."

"Let's cruise, I've got a meeting in the dining room." Don was already in a jogging suit and was lacing up his hiking boots. He sauntered down the hall without bothering to see if they were coming. Lucy hurled Serena a glare. When they reached the dining room, Don was already sitting at the front table with two men. Lucy took the chair to his left. Don made no effort to introduce anyone, Lucy leaned towards the two men and extended a hand.

"Lucy Whitman. Delighted to meet you. So are you two gentlemen followers of Masterji?"

"We're film-makers."

"Oh, how marvellous!"

"We're talking about a new project," said Don.

"You mean helping Sam?" asked Serena.

"No, a film, I would imagine." Lucy kicked Serena under the table, how dumb the girl could be. The film-makers posed questions to Don. Lucy studied the menu. Serena fiddled with a teaspoon. Sam walked past the table, carrying an accordian.

"Hey, where'd you get that?" asked Don.

"At Baja's."

"Can I check it out?"

"It's for Ramesh."

"Who's Ramesh?"

"He's the cook."

"Can I just take a look?"

Sam stared at Don, then handed him the accordian. Don slung the strap over his shoulder, pressed the keys, tried and failed to make any sound come out of it. Ramesh came over to the table with two plates of toast. Sam whispered to Ramesh in rapid Hindi.

"Wow, you can really speak that stuff." Don flashed his preternaturally brilliant movie star smile. Sam blinked indifferently and continued talking with Ramesh. Lucy caught Don's turquoise eyes (were they contact lenses?) taking an inventory of Sam's torso and legs, which were partially visible, due to the black pants she was wearing.

"Hey, can we borrow this for a jam session?"

"You'll have to ask Ramesh." Sam took the accordian and followed Ramesh into the kitchen.

"Donny, that's the girl I was telling you about," Lucy whispered.

"What girl?"

"She's the one we're trying to help. She's part of our group but the poor thing is destitute and sleeping in the linen closet! We want her to stay in a good room like everyone else."

"Can you make a contribution? The Rolfs made one this morning," Serena added. Lucy gouged Serena's thigh under the table.

"Interesting," Don nodded at the kitchen door as if it bequeathed some special insight.

Masterji's cold grew worse so there was no teaching in the afternoon. Anu made Shanti and Amla dry two extra loads of laundry. Alicia, James, Serena, Lucy and the Rolfs assembled in the rose arbor behind the Khanna's house to read. Lucy put aside her book and dozed off when some very loud and irritating music erupted from the servants quarters. Lucy marched in its direction, ready to put whoever was making it promptly in their place, kicked open the gate and saw Sam, Chintu, Gobind, Ramesh and several ragged children sitting in a circle playing tablas, flute, accordian and bongos. Don wasn't there but his guitar was and Sam was playing it.

Chintu held up a harmonica, "Join in, man."

"Oh, well, it's just terrific, but the others over in the garden are finding it a tad loud..."

"Tell them to go sit on the front porch, they won't hear it there." said Sam.

"But we have been sitting in the rose garden for some time prior to you..." Don, in a red kurta and Kulu cap, sat beside Sam and began playing the harmonica. Gobind and Sam sang in Hindi. Lucy tried to remain calm, after all Don was a performer and he was performing. The music swelled, belittling and ignoring her. She wondered if she should or could join in, and if not, what she should say to Don at dinner.

Sam heard a knock, opened the door and saw Lucy, Serena, Alicia and George crouched in the hall. Sam handed out pillows, everyone managed to fit on the floor and bed. It wasn't quite how Lucy had planned it, everyone was squeezed together, rain drummed on the tin roof, dampness seeped through the floor. Yet the little room was surprisingly warm, Sam had decorated it with Gujarati shawls and religious calendar posters, a stick of incense burned before a small clay icon of Ganesh and a faded photograph of Masterji and Mahatma Gandhi. It was more intimate than the other rooms in the guest house, which didn't have enough rugs, pictures or furniture.

Sam knelt at the head of the bed and lit a *bidi*. "Does anyone want tea?"

"Oh no, we mustn't trouble you..." said Lucy.

"It doesn't take long, I can make coffee too." Sam

reached for tins of sugar, tea and coffee which were stored on a small shelf above a hot plate.

"That isn't why we've come, it's well—we're all rather concerned about you."

Sam put down her tins and stared at Lucy. Lucy feigned a cough and glanced about for support. No one moved, she took the floor. "We realise it must be difficult for you to live in this little room while the rest of us have so much space, so we all got together and thought about it and decided that in the spirit of Masterji's teachings, we want you to have a decent room like everyone else, so we've all pitched in to pay for it. I've spoken with Mrs Khanna and she said there's a room available as of tomorrow." Lucy smiled beneficently and spread her shawl over her knees, like a queen bequeathing treasure. Serena, George and Alicia turned to Sam, who stared back at Lucy. Lucy twitched and wondered what to do next. "We just thought that if we were all closer together we could really practice what Masterji says and share everything we're learning and experiencing."

"How much money is it?"

"How much? Oh, you mustn't worry about that dear..."

"I'm curious, how much is it?"

"It's, it's... gosh, I really don't know, but we've all got plenty, don't you think twice, for us it isn't much at all."

"But it's at least a couple of hundred dollars, correct?"

"Yes, about that."

"I'd prefer it if you gave the money to Ramesh. He needs to buy dowries for his daughters."

George and Alicia exchanged glances, Serena studied her fingers, interlaced in her lap. "We really intended the money for you," said George.

"I understand, but as you can see I don't need it. The Khannas let me stay in this room and I like it here. I like to be close to Ramesh and Shanti because they're my friends. I don't suppose any of you are aware of how hard they work and how little they earn. People think that if Indians have employment, any kind of employment, they're not starving and they don't have any problems. But Ramesh has six daughters all of whom need dowries, and even though he works seven days a week, he can't earn enough to buy dowries for each of them. His oldest daughter Amla is eighteen and she's not engaged yet, which is a big problem."

George cleared his throat and repositioned himself on the bed. "But the dowry system is terrible and I don't think we should support it."

"That's right!" cried Lucy. "Buying dowries only makes for more trouble. It really isn't a good idea, don't you agree, Alicia, Serena? You're women, you wouldn't want to be sold into marriage to a perfect stranger, would you?" Serena and Alicia nodded.

"If you intended the money for me, why can't I do what I want with it?"

"I think it's wonderful that you want to help these people," said Alicia, "but I think it makes more sense to support organisations like UNICEF."

Sam leaned back on the bed, her arms crossed behind her head. "You don't know what the hell you're talking about. The dowry system is horrible, obviously, but the outrage of rich white people doesn't change a fucking thing, neither do reports published in Ford Foundation newsletters or protest marches with upper class Delhi feminists hoisting their Down With Dowry signs. If you're a poor Indian girl, you're going to have your marriage arranged and if your parents don't have the requisite dowry, the chances of getting into a halfway decent situation are very slim. If you really want to help someone who's poor just give them your money. Sending checks to Save the Children or UNICEF pays salaries for more rich white people to write reports about how starvation kills people. Who the hell cares what happens in the long run when reality, and that means 'no dowry, no future', is staring you in the face? But I can see that you'd rather pay for another American to stay in a large room for a few weeks than help Amla have a decent life."

"We came here to help you and you lecture us about charity and poverty!" Lucy shouted.

"Get out of my room."

"What?"

"Would you get out of my room, please?" No one moved, Sam kicked open the door and ran out. The sugar tin spilled over the hot plate.

"Well, I'm never going to try that again!" Lucy sputtered. "It just goes to show it's impossible to help people. They simply don't understand, they get demanding and difficult and everything ends up worse than it was. Anyway, their bad lot is their own bad karma, so why interfere. Really, I could just . . . oh!" Lucy pushed her white cashmere shawl over her shoulder and marched upstairs. Alicia, George and Serena shuffled single-file into the garden. George pulled a rose blossom from a trellis and spun it in his fingers.

"I suppose we should've asked her if she wanted a bigger room in the first place."

"She's just one of those difficult characters." Serena wound an arm around George's waist and lay her head on his shoulder. The rain had ended, nets of mist clung to the rhododendron bushes.

"She's right," said Alicia. "We're perfectly happy to let these people wait on us while we read holy books and feel so special."

"But, but they are getting paid to do it."

"Yes, but we treat them like servants."

"Things are different here. Being a servant isn't so bad in India, it's a pretty good job."

"But it's still being a servant."

George pulled away from Serena and leaned into the fence with one foot on the rail and both hands around a stalk of morning glory. "It'll be awfully tense around here until this thing blows over."

The wind had stripped the blossoms from all the apple trees, the birds were driven under rocks, black clouds hovered against the mountains. A dog moaned in the bush, which reminded Sam that everyone was wet and cold, nobody was having a good time. The shepherd family that lived in the hut below the orchard didn't even have a tin roof, just mismatched slabs of wood from old packing crates. Sam had never wanted time to pass so quickly, especially in India where each hour was precious. To endure the rest of the teachings with those people, who were so clearly against her, for what reason she couldn't understand, to have to wait for Masterji's decision . . . tomorrow it would be twenty-five more days, then it would be nineteen more days, then fifteen, then ten . . . but today it was twenty-six, which was unbearable. She wanted to cry, but that would be selfish, giving in to a deluded notion of the self, everything Masterji had spoken of two days ago. The relentlessly awful weather was a lesson in patience and self-control, an opportunity to apply the lessons of the teachings. Sam squeezed her eyes shut and repeated a mantra over and over until the syllables dissolved into meaningless sounds. Finally, gratefully, she gave into tears, crouched against the tree and sobbed into her knees.

The next afternoon, the sky was leaden and dull, like the November sky in Manhattan. For some reason it made Alicia remember her mother's apartment, a series of cavernous rooms on Fifth Avenue upon which so much time, money and effort had been expended that everyone was afraid to use them. She had spent so many hours lying on the red sofa in the library, staring onto the street below, wondering when and how she would find true love. She was fiercely committed to the ideal, though she had never come near to finding anyone who could give it to her. She knew that she gave the impression of being disinterested, even as she studied the eyes and hands of every man she met. When she was a girl, the other children always gathered around her, but at some point her wealth made her retreat. Elusive, vague and unreliable were charges frequently made against her; she exasperated her friends, she knew. She knew she gave the impression of not needing or wanting anyone, it was a vestigal defense from her childhood, which, now that she was almost thirty, had stranded her.

She lay across the ground, her eyes half closed, pressing into damp earth and leaves, feeling traces of cold air on her legs and hands. She imagined Masterji as a young man. His hair would have been dark, his eyes would not have changed, but maybe he wouldn't have been as remote as he was now, he would have had passions, dislikes, wounds, desires. Somehow, his detachment angered her, though she knew that she could not trust him if he behaved otherwise. She wanted his attention, she wanted to be singled out, to be acknowledged, to have him listen to her, analyse her. She was ashamed to admit that she was jealous of the other foreigners, she needed Masterji more than they did. She wondered how it would feel to be alone with him, if, when she had the full force of his attention, he would simply praise her, or, perhaps, not praise her or touch her, but demand even more of her. If the disciple was supposed to surrender to the guru, then the guru should grant the disciple his devotion. It should be, then, like falling in love. She heard branches cracking and bolted upright—it was Prem collecting firewood.

"Come inside, have some tea."

Alicia followed Prem into his room at the back of the school. The room was spare, with a few very beautifully made rugs, a desk and a sideboard with four engraved silver frames which displayed black and white photographs of Prem's relatives. Two men from the village came in. Prem gave them tea and cigarettes, they asked him to read some letters. The younger man opened a notebook, Prem helped him write a sentence. The men finished their tea and cigarettes and left.

"I'm sorry that took so long. I never turn these fellows away when they need help with reading or writing. If they can read labels on parcels and boxes they don't get cheated by shopkeepers."

"Does that happen often?"

"Oh yes, all the time."

"How many adult students do you have?"

"I don't really know, I just help as many people as I can. The servants and labourers don't have a lot of time, so we put in short lessons here and there. When the guest house is full, they have to get up at seven and work till eleven."

"Does your family have servants?"

"Of course, I grew up with them. After my parents they're the first people I call on when I go back to Delhi." Their hands brushed as Alicia reached for the plate of apricots. She felt a blush spreading over her cheeks. She could sense, as she always did with men, that he found her attractive. She wondered if he was lonely living in the mountains with only the Khannas and the school, if he had or wanted a girlfriend.

"Someone told me you were a writer."

"I used to write poetry," Alicia blushed again.

"But you don't anymore?"

"I felt that it was irrelevant, so I tried to work in politics. I got disillusioned with that too. The only thing anyone wanted me for was fund-raising."

"Have you discussed this with Masterji?"

"No, I've never discussed anything with Masterji."

"He's very good at helping people find the right kind of

work. He told me to run the school and the orphanage, which saved me from going into my family business. That young man who was just here is Ramesh's nephew. His family's had a very hard time: the father abandoned them, the mother's too ill to work. He's determined to learn to read and he's making real progress. He'll be literate in a few months, then I can help him get a better job. The smallest amount of money makes a huge difference to a family, a lot of the people around here make less than fifty dollars a year." Prem rolled tobacco into a cigarette paper. Alicia noticed his long eyelashes.

"Do you ever miss living in a city?"

"Sometimes, yes. I miss going to friends' houses, music concerts. A lot of people pass through the guest house so I have some idea what's going on outside of Devigunj." He offered her a cigarette, she accepted, though she didn't smoke. Sam ran into the room, saw Alicia, and froze.

"Join us, we're just having some tea and cigarettes."

"I—I can't, I just wanted to borrow your dictionary for a minute." Sam clutched the book to her chest and ran out. Prem watched from the door.

"Have you known her for some time?" asked Alicia.

"Oh, yes. She seems upset these days, she used to be so happy. I've always admired the way she befriends the villagers, I've never seen a foreigner speak Hindi the way she does." Shanti entered with a tray of tea and sandwiches. She smiled at Alicia; Prem asked her to sit, she shook her head, smiled once more at Alicia and left. Alicia saw that Shanti didn't have any socks or a raincoat. She looked down at her own five-hundred-dollar boots and was ashamed.

Serena lay on the bed, unable to read or to sleep. George sat by the window, his prayer book open on his lap, his mouth shaping the Sanskrit syllables, his eyes staring at the page. Serena pounded her pillow and screamed.

"You've left me. You're gone. We'll never get married, never..."

George finished his prayers, sat on the bed, and tried to hold Serena's hand. "Serena, I'm not leaving you..."

"You'll do whatever Masterji tells you to. The other day I heard you say nothing was more important than the path. What did you mean by that?"

"These bodies are impermanent, we'll soon leave them, we'll die, and when we die only our practice and our guru can save us, not our friends, not our love for each other..."

"Stop it, I can't listen to this!" Serena grabbed her coat, ran into the garden and up the hill towards the Shiva temple. She tripped on a rock and heard a shriek, got to her feet, wiped the mud off her hands and knees and saw a small rodent bleeding on a rock. Blood and intestines seeped from its stomach. It gasped for breath, its paws clawed the air. It looked directly at her, as if pleading for help, then it fell against the rock and lay still. Serena touched it, blood still poured from its stomach but its face and paws went stiff. Serena remembered Masterji saying that when an animal died one should chant a mantra in its ear so it could take a human birth, but Serena couldn't remember any mantras and the creature was already dead. She started to vomit. The rain came harder, she held onto a rock to keep from sliding into the ravine. When she reached the top of the hill she ran towards the temple and crashed on the floor. Sam sat near the *lingam*, painting a watercolour.

"What happened?"

"I just killed something, I didn't mean to, I didn't!" Serena shrieked, rain and mud dripped from her hair and her blue overcoat.

"What was it?"

"I don't know, a chipmunk or a rat or something, I tripped and fell on it, it was an accident, I swear, I didn't mean to kill it, I didn't!"

"We kill things all the time just by breathing and walking."

"But I saw it die! Masterji said at one of the teachings that when you take life, even by accident, you get bad karma, but I don't understand all this talk about karma and reincarnation, I don't and I don't want to!" Serena threw herself into Sam's lap and screamed. Sam didn't know how to comfort her, there was nothing comforting to say, life was terrifying and dismal, she'd arrived at that very conclusion moments ago. She stroked Serena's hair, the rain tapered into a slow drizzle, Serena sniffled quietly in Sam's lap, Sam got Serena to her feet and steered her down the trail, to her little room by the laundry. Serena lay on Sam's bed while Sam put a fresh kettle of water on the hot plate.

"You like it here, don't you."

"Yes, unfortunately. I can't live in America."

"Why not?"

"I find it grim, ugly and impoverished."

"That's what most people say about India."

"I know, I know. I gave up trying to explain myself long ago."

"Have you ever been in love?"

"Oh yes."

"What happened?"

"I was sent to college in America, he went to art school in England. Neither of us had any money so we could only meet once or twice a year."

"Is it too late?"

"Yes. He's married."

"Do you want to get married?"

"It isn't something I expect will happen. Do you want to marry George?"

"Of course, but Masterji's going to pick him for the initiation! Masterji is his whole life, everything Masterji says he just . . ."

"If Masterji picks him, and I agree, I think he will, in a year or two you'll be relieved that you didn't marry George. I know that's the last thing you want to hear right now, but trust me, it becomes exhausting, wanting someone who doesn't want you." Sam poured hot water into the teapot. Rain tapped on the tin roof, the thin cry of a jackal echoed from the woods.

"Why did you come here?"

"Because I've reached a crisis. I'm thirty, I don't have a profession or a husband. I don't have any money. I'm an American citizen but I loathe America. I came here because I have nowhere else to go. As long as the teachings go on I can sleep in this room. When they're over I don't know what I'll do."

"I hope Masterji picks you so you can stay in India."

"I don't really care about that. I don't hope for anything anymore. I think you should get out of here. The weather's disgusting and you are not interested in the teachings. Go back to the States."

"But what about George?"

"It'll be good for him. He'll miss you."

"May I come in?" Alicia stood at the door. Sam and Serena stared, then Sam lowered her head and reached for the teapot.

"I've been thinking about the conversation we had the other day... I'm sorry if we offended you."

"Don't worry about it." Sam passed Alicia a teacup without looking up.

"Since we did collect the money for you, I think you should do what you like with it—you know—give it to Ramesh for his daughters."

"How much is it?"

Alicia handed Sam an envelope. Sam shook out the bills and counted them. "It's not enough for all six girls. Can you get more?"

"You're sure it isn't enough?"

"Yes, I'm sure. Go ask Ramesh."

"If we raise more money how would we know that he'll use it for the dowries?"

"I can get receipts. It's not a lot of money for people like you. I've already given them everything I can."

Alicia's eyes scrutinised the room for hidden assets, but there really was nothing but a few books and an old camera.

"I'll give you the rest." Serena piled a crumpled stack of rupees and dollar bills on Sam's pillow—her mother had trained her never to leave money in hotel rooms. "Take this too," she unhooked a thin gold necklace and put it on the pile. Alicia paused, opened her wallet and withdrew several crisp hundred-dollar bills which she lay at Sam's knees. Sam counted the money.

"You just saved eight lives."

"Eight?"

"That's counting Ramesh and Shanti, the girls' parents."

"Well, I'm—I'm glad."

"Let's go give it to them right now." Sam led Serena and Alicia to Ramesh and Shanti's hut behind the kitchen. Amla and Roopa were crouched by the stove when Serena and Alicia came in. Sam spoke quietly in Hindi, handed Amla the envelope and pointed to Serena and Alicia. Alma and Roopa sobbed and hugged Sam, then touched Serena and Alicia's feet.

"Can I come in? I'm out of aspirin and hairspray." Sanjal stood at Lucy's door in a blue silk sari, high-heeled sandals and sunglasses.

"Oh Sanjal, have you heard the latest? The Rolfs had a second private audience and immediately left for Delhi! That means two down, nine to go! The stakes are certainly getting higher. Why are you so dressed up in the middle of the afternoon?"

"I had to dress for my interview."

"What interview?"

"My interview with Masterji."

"You mean you had a private audience?"

"Oh yes, totally private. Prem sat in the hallway." Sanjal toyed with Lucy's electric hairdryer.

"How did you ever get one? I've been trying for weeks!"

"Jodi arranged it. It was very uplifting." Sanjal yawned and stretched a jewelled hand towards the lipsticks stacked against the mirror. "He also advised against rushing into a new marriage, he said my meditation should come first."

"That's what I need help with. I've got to figure out when and how to divorce Damion! Dammit!" Lucy threw her nail file against the wall.

Sanjal drew a red leather jacket from Lucy's closet. "What a super coat."

"Oh take it, I never use it."

"And such nice jewellery." Sanjal tried on various earrings, necklaces and bangles, turned and paused before the mirror, admired her skin, her brows and eyelashes, the way her bosom brought out the turquoise sheen of her sari blouse, raised her arms to take another look at the taut line of muscle that ran from the chest to the hip. "Is this your husband?" Sanjal lifted a photograph from the dresser.

"No, that's my friend Victor, he introduced me to Masterji. You'd adore him, he holds Dakini workshops and runs an art gallery on King's Road. You and Dipali must come stay with me, I insist."

"Dipali never goes out of India. Can I really keep it?"

"Yes, of course. But aren't we supposed to stop wearing leathers and furs? Prem said Masterji would be offended if I wore my fox coat to the teachings. I must admit, I have been tempted to pull it out a thousand times, the weather's so gruesome."

"Just stop eating meat for some time and the karma will reverse." Sanjal pulled Lucy's comb through her hair, poised her sunglasses on top of her head and turned up the jacket collar.

"Looks good." Don Williams grinned from the doorway.

Jodi was about to turn out the living room lights and go upstairs to Sanjal's room when Lucy tapped his shoulder.

"Jodi darling, can you spare a moment?"

"Of course, sit down." Flustered, Jodi automatically poured a scotch, assuming she wanted his drink.

"No thanks, dearie, you have it." Lucy caressed his hand and pulled herself close. She smelled of American chemicals, like an airplane or a hotel bathroom.

"I just feel so confused about balancing the spiritual and the physical sides of life, I've got to ask Masterji for some advice. Actually, I will have a sip." She took the glass and dipped her finger into Jodi's glass. Jodi poured more whiskey, her gargoyle eyes were too alarming to be viewed at close range.

"... so I told Damion he'd have to move out if he didn't start painting again. He wasn't a bad painter, he was actually rather good..." Jodi tried to block out what she was saying while nodding at what he guessed were the appropriate moments.

"Jodi, have you got a headache? You're acting very peculiar."

"No, no, its—it's rather cold, shall we go to your room?"

"Good thinking, I am a tad chilly." Lucy wound her arms around Jodi's waist and led him upstairs. He hoped they'd pass Sanjal's room so he could look in but Lucy rushed him up the back stairs, bolted the door and pulled Jodi onto her couch. Jodi didn't understand what she was leading up to, if it was what he suspected, he'd have to swallow more whiskey to get it over with.

"Jodi, I've got to talk to Masterji right away. I've been waiting for weeks. I asked Prem the first day I arrived. The

Rolfs and Sanjal and George have had their audiences. It simply isn't fair!"

"I'll arrange one for you tomorrow." He was relieved, an audience with Masterji was all she wanted, but the whiskey had softened his vision and will power, he slid one arm around her shoulder and moved the other towards her thigh.

"I'm coming round at nine to make sure you won't forget. I've got to wear something perfect, something serious and elegant... how does one ever compete with a sari?" Lucy pulled jackets, sweaters and pants off hangers and posed before the mirror. She was probably a sack of wrinkles under her ludicrous pink sweater, nevertheless, here they were, and what did she think she was doing, inviting him to her bedroom at 11.30? He swallowed another half a glass of whiskey, came up behind her and slid both hands around her waist.

"Goodness, you startled me." She nudged him aside and tried on a fringed purple jacket. "Is this too Knightsbridgy for Masterji? I don't want him to think that I'm overly interested in clothes."

"You always look very elegant."

"Really?" Lucy flushed with pride. "I'm so glad you think so because I do make my best effort. There's no getting away from it, clothes matter. "

"Women today have forgotten the power of dressing..." Before Jodi decided on his next move, Lucy's tongue was in his mouth and her hands on his neck. He lost his balance and fell back on the bed. Lucy pulled off her sweater, her pink lace bodice held in loose, freckled skin, and Jodi was besieged with hallucinations of the pallid New Zealander. He heard giggling and scuffling in the hallway. It couldn't be George and Serena, they were always in bed by ten. May be it was Sanjal or Don. He bolted upright.

"Have you got aspirin?"

"Wouldn't you rather have codeine?" Jodi saw the skin under her arm quiver as she reached for a pillbox on the dresser, again he smelled deodorant and face cream.

"I'd better get some sleep or I won't be up in time to book your audience."

"Jodi, you're a positive angel." She seized his head and pressed her mouth over his in what he assumed was a kiss. He managed to get through the door, he wanted to go down the hall to Sanjal's room but Lucy winked and blew kisses from her doorway, so he stumbled quickly down the stairs.

Lucy arrived promptly at nine to secure Jodi's promise of a private audience in two days' time. She resolved not to tell anyone, not even Sanjal, she knew they'd all be jealous and try to stop it.

Alicia, George and Serena were finishing breakfast when Lucy and Don came in.

"Oh, the things we saw. Divine little temples, and do you know they've got mongooses around here! How authentically Indian can you get! Hello, what's this?"

Shanti and Ramesh hovered near the kitchen door, holding baskets of flower garlands and sweets. They came forward shyly, put the garlands around Serena and Alicia's necks, touched their feet. Shanti seized Alicia's legs and sobbed, "Thank you, memsahib, thank you, memsahib." Ramesh bowed and wept, his eyes lowered, his hands pressed to his heart. Serena and Alicia pulled Ramesh and Shanti to their feet and hugged them, Shanti and Ramesh returned to the kitchen, tears still streaming down their faces.

"What was that all about?" Lucy pushed her sunglasses onto her forehead and squinted towards the kitchen.

"That's Ramesh and his wife Shanti, the ones with the six daughters," said Alicia

"Don't tell me you gave into that Sam and bought the dowries!"

"We did, but I wouldn't call it 'giving in'."

"That is precisely what it is, and it is perpetuating everything that's wrong with India!" Lucy's cheeks flamed. "And that selfish, impossible Sam creature, you listened to her?"

"I think she's nice," said Serena.

"She has no manners and she's a freeloader. Just ask Mrs Khanna about her."

"We'd be hypocrites to take back the money we raised for her because she wanted to use it for something other than the room. If you think Sam's room is small, you should see how small the servant's house is."

"You should've consulted with me, the whole thing was my idea in the first place!"

"I'll pay you for your share if you like." Alicia threw her wallet on the table.

"Heavens, what do you take me for? Come on, Don, let's go." Lucy stuffed her camera and hairbrush into her purse.

"I think it's great what you guys did." Don balanced his enormous green cowboy boots on the edge of the table. "That's what Masterji's message is all about." Don grinned at Alicia, Lucy swiftly lowered herself back into her chair.

"Mrs Khanna, I've got to talk to you." Lucy tiptoed into the kitchen where Anu was boiling jars for her homemade apple-lemon chutney which she expected would win the first prize at the Himachal Ladies Community-Funding Drive.

"Of course, of course. Please have some tea, I've just made it. Aren't you looking smart this afternoon!"

"I'm finally having my private audience with Masterji. Your darling husband arranged it, he's so divinely considerate." Lucy had decided, after several hours before the mirror, on a black wool suit, a green scarf pinned around her neck with a diamond brooch, her hair brushed into two gilded planes instead of a French knot.

"Oh yes, Mr Khanna is always thinking of the guests' needs." Anu turned the jars over with plastic tongs, while taking surreptitious tally of the possible number of karats in Lucy's diamonds.

"I hate to be the one to bring up any sort of unpleasantness, but you run such a super show here I feel I've just got to break the news." Lucy patted her hair and earrings into place and fixed her enormous eyes on Anu. "One of my necklaces is missing, a very special piece with blue sapphires. I found out this morning when I was sorting through my effects. In thirty years of travel I've never lost a single piece of jewellery except for a few rings left in washbasins, which is altogether different. This necklace was either around my neck or in my special pouch, so I know someone must have stolen it. Now, I feel I must also tell you that this morning I saw Serena's gold necklace on the girl who sweeps my room."

"Which one?"

"I don't know the names, I believe she's one of the dowry cases Sam's foisted on us."

"What dowry case?"

"Didn't you know? That Sam is pressuring us to buy dowries for the cook's family. Naturally we all want to help and she's put us in a spot because we don't want to support the dowry system. In my opinion, these girls work for you, so you're the one who ought to call the shots, not the little welfare case in peasant skirts you've so sweetly taken in. I don't know how that girl got Serena's necklace but it must be looked into. Oh gosh, it's time to head up to Masterji's, I've got a thousand questions for him. Do let me know if I can be of help, I know how difficult it is to get good staff." Lucy kissed Anu on both cheeks and tiptoed out of the door. Anu turned off the stove, tucked her key ring under her sari and marched towards the servants' quarters.

Jodi went to Dehradun on the pretext of finding some special parts for his jeep, assailed by visions of Sanjal with Don Williams. He returned well after dinner when he knew Anu would be asleep, took a quick shower, put on a silk *kurta pyjama* and went into the guest house.

"Sanjal?" Jodi nudged Sanajal's door. The room was empty, though there were signs of recent passing, overloaded ashtrays, fresh odours of tobacco and perfume, eruptions of scarves, pants, shoes and cosmetic bottles from the four suitcases. Maybe she was sleeping in Dipali's room, but there wasn't enough space, with the two *aiyas*, the children and Dipali, all on three mattresses. Could she have gone to Lucy's room? Possibly, and if so, he could go wake her up. He went down the hall, the old wood squeaking under his feet. Lucy's door was half an inch out of its frame. He touched it lightly, it swung open. Lucy was snoring loudly, hair in curlers. He went to Don's room and pressed his ear against the door. He heard music, the creak of wood and brass, Sanjal's unmistakable giggle. He ran down the stairs and out of the door, his *kurta* caught on the fence and ripped. He cursed, stubbed three toes, got the door open, went straight to his bed, seething at the thought of Sanjal with that large, unwashed, unintelligible American in sweat pants. He'd never seen one of the creature's movies. Anu continually fussed over him, paid special attention to his food, invited him to dinner. The man had no manners, he belched, put his boots against the table to push back his chair. Now Sanjal was in bed with him, putting on quite a show, no doubt. She hadn't made much effort for Jodi; as soon as it was over she lunged for the bourbon and cigarettes and acted as if they'd just come out of a movie. At 3.30, after two sleeping pills and half a pint of gin, Jodi was able to shut his eyes.

"Jodi, you must speak to Sam. She's created a huge disturbance among the guests." Anu flung the curtains open.

Jodi groaned and heaved a blanket over his eyes. "She solicited funds from the other guests to buy dowries for the servant's daughters. This time she's really gone too far, you have to do something." When Anu was annoyed her face gained five pounds in fullness and ten years in age. Jodi lifted his head half an inch and gasped in pain.

"Jodi, what is the matter with you?"

"I've got a headache." If Anu suspected him of drinking she never mentioned it, her marriage was predicated on the denial of the possibility of her husband enjoying himself anywhere but at her dining table.

"We've been feeding Sam for two months and she hasn't paid anything."

"She gave us three of her paintings and they're the best things in this whole place. Get me some Disprin, will you?" Anu swiftly produced a tray with Disprin and ice water. She'd painted her nails fluorescent pink, which looked absurd in a place like Devigunj. Anu's glare made it clear there would be no peace in the house unless he moved.

"Alright, I'll go see what's up." Jodi pulled himself upright and pushed his feet into slippers.

"You're going out in pyjamas?"

"Can't you see that I'm ill for Godsakes? I'm only doing this because you insist, oh hell . . ." His temples throbbed hideously. He put on his sunglasses and headed towards the guest house. He knew Anu disapproved of Sam's wilful violations of acceptable feminine conduct, he admired the way Sam would talk and drink and smoke with anyone. He heard the sound of wails and footsteps from the kitchen; he saw Shanti sobbing wildly in Sam's lap; George, Alicia and Serena hovering by the pantry.

"What's going on in here, Sam?"

"Amla's run away. She was upset by all the trouble she'd caused about her dowry."

"Can I talk to you for a moment?" Jodi beckoned to

Sam, who put Shanti into Serena's lap and followed Jodi outside. "Sam, how could you let this happen?"

"Lucy started it. She got this idea that I should stay in a big room and made the others give money. I said I didn't need it, I wanted to give it to Ramesh and Shanti for the girls. She's mad about it, yesterday she accused Amla of stealing a necklace."

"How did I miss all of this?"

"You look like you've got a hangover."

"I do. I feel like hell."

"Try this." Sam handed Jodi a packet of black pills. "Tibetan medicine. It tastes bad but it works. So do headstands and *pranayama*."

"Acht, that Lucy woman. Where does Masterji pick them up?" Jodi chewed three pills, grimaced and swallowed. "Tastes disgusting. Do you think Amla did it? These rich women leave crores worth of stuff lying about their rooms."

"In all the years you've known Ramesh's family, have they ever stolen anything? Or lied to you?"

"No."

"They've never complained about their quarters or their salaries either."

"So what do we do?"

"Search for Amla. It'll be hard because the rain's about to start again."

"I'll go round up some cars." Jodi went to the dining room, opened the door and reeled. There she was, sitting between Don and the ridiculous little Punjabi film-maker with his absurd black hat cocked over his left eye. She was carrying on, hands and legs all over the place, showing off for Don, who, as expected, was wearing dirty sweat pants and a tee-shirt, with one leg bobbing up and down and the other pushed against the table. He was practically exhibiting his testicles, his legs were spread so far apart, then again it was what he did for a living.

"Oh, Jodi, come sit with us. Chintu, get a chair." Sanjal pushed Chintu off his seat.

"Don't bother."

"So then my uncle, the former foreign minister, he could hardly stand up, he had so much booze in him, he goes up to the Soviet Ambassador and speaks in German . . ." Sanjal howled and slapped Don's thigh. Jodi tossed his unlit cigarette on the floor and stormed out.

"Where's Jodi gone? I was coming to the punch line."

Lucy slid into the chair beside Don. "Sanjal, tell that cook to get me some tea post-haste."

"Lucy, you don't look well at all, what's up?"

"I'm not. I was supposed to have my private audience with Masterji but he cancelled on account of his cold. I must have stockpiles of bad karma from all sorts of dreadful past lives."

Sanjal caressed the necklace that rolled over her breasts. "Don, you were very lucky to get your audience before Masterji's illness increased." Don smiled and stuck a toothpick into his gums.

"You didn't tell me you had an audience!" Lucy drew her chair up to Don's, but Don started walking out, with Sanjal and Chintu following.

Two days passed without any sign of Amla. Sam and Alicia kept a vigil in Ramesh and Shanti's hut. Three days passed with no clue. Shanti exhausted herself from crying. Alicia and Sam went to Shanti's hut to cajole her to eat some food. Shanti sat by the family shrine, next to the stove, murmuring incoherently and beating her fists against her chest and forehead. She opened her strongbox, took out a roll of rupees and a silver talisman and ran her hands over Alicia's forehead.

"What's she saying?"

"She wants you to take it to the temple for her. She says

you saved her daughter's life once, so the Goddess will listen to you. Go to the Durga temple, that one just above the town. Buy some flowers and sweets at the stall in the front, take them inside and offer them to the Goddess. And pray for Amla."

Shanti tied the talisman around Alicia's neck, knelt by the shrine and lay down with her face in her arms. Alicia started down the hill. The temple had just opened for evening darshan. She bought two garlands of roses and marigolds and a plate of sweets, removed her boots and went inside. An aged *pujari* sat behind a wooden desk, clutching a staff in one hand and a prayer book in the other, his voice turned over the Sanskrit syllables in a gentle, rhythmic lilt, like water in a stream. The central idol was an enormous, crudely painted ten-armed goddess astride a tiger. Two mice ran under the tiger's tail, a line of ants moved over the trail of crushed sweets that led from the *pujari* to a small strongbox. The idol looked so incongruously dramatic in the hushed concrete room, with the old man murmuring quietly and the ants and mice moving across the floor. Alicia went over to the *pujari* and held out the flowers and sweets. He motioned to her to sit, poured some water into her palms and signalled her to drink it. She pretended to swallow, and let it trickle through her fingers onto her lap. The old man rubbed red powder on her forehead, took the garlands and flung them across the floor, held the sweets towards the goddess, then handed them back to her and waved her away.

Alicia was halfway up the hill when she realised she'd forgotten to pray for Amla. She wondered whether to kneel on the ground with her hands clasped, but that felt wrong, she had to find another temple or shrine of some kind. She saw a leper with a makeshift shrine and a tiffin laid out to receive alms. She dropped a few rupee notes into the tiffin, joined her hands and prayed for Amla. The leper lifted an arm and moaned. There was no nose or fingers, the body was so deformed she couldn't tell if it was a man or a woman's. She'd passed so many lepers on so many of her walks, usually she left a few coins or just looked away, but for some reason she felt that she had to do something for this one. She wondered whether she should bring food or whether she should take him/her to some place dry and warm. The leper couldn't walk, the legs were too shrivelled, and she was afraid to carry him/her. There was a small clinic in Devigunj but it only administered medicines, and Anu would never permit a leper anywhere near the guest house. She flagged a taxi, picked up the leper and told the driver to go to the Durga temple. The driver was horrified. Alicia yelled at him and waved a stack of rupees. He sped down the hill, nearly collided with a bus as he pulled up to the temple. Alicia tossed him the money, went inside the temple and sat on the floor with the leper still in her arms.

To her surprise the leper did not squirm, but lay gently in her lap, like a child. After several minutes the eyes looked into her face. They were clogged with mucus and dirt, the disease having eaten away most of the nose and lips. Alicia wondered if she might contract the disease and if so what she should do about it. The leper lifted a stub of what remained of the hand and moaned again. Alicia carried the leper to the *pujari* to ask for a blessing. The pujari looked up from his prayer-book, adjusted his glasses and saw the leper on Alicia's lap. He screamed and swatted Alicia with his staff. The mice darted under the idol, Alicia shouted, the *pujari* kicked her and shrieked again. Alicia carried the leper out to the road and collapsed on the ground. The leper took the tiffin and hobbled away from her. She went after him but he waved a stump at her, angrily, it seemed, and moved quickly down the road. Alicia's mind reeled with memories of her childhood, her mother and father screaming, her mother beating her with hairbrushes and shoes, the corridors of hated boarding schools, holidays with indifferent grandparents and cousins. She couldn't understand why these memories had emerged when she felt the tender weight of the leper on her lap. She wished the leper hadn't left her alone on the roadside, she clutched her stomach, and prayed that the leper would come back for her.

She ran down the hill, searching for the leper. The road wound into a garden filled with gigantic painted idols enclosed in chain-link fences. Monkeys and vultures scattered and there was a sour smell of decaying food and rodents. Her boot got stuck in a hole, she pulled it out and nearly fell over. She saw more monkeys and rats, she heard a burst of drums and cries, it sounded like something was being sacrificed or beaten, then it died as suddenly as it had begun.

A car knocked her sideways. She tumbled on the asphalt and hit a tree. She felt blood on her face, her fingers found the string that had held the talisman, which was now gone. When she was able to stand up she felt all the limbs in place—nothing was broken. She managed to make it up to the road, to the edge of Anu's garden. She leaned on the gate and stared up the hillside, into the window of the room where Masterji was sleeping.

At midnight Prem opened the door of Ramesh and Shanti's hut. "I've found Amla. She's outside in my jeep. I saw her at the train station in Haridwar."

"Did anything happen to her?" asked Sam.

"No, no, she's alright. She spent two nights at a *dharamsala* in Haridwar."

"How'd she get there?"

"She walked halfway, then took a bus. Thank God I saw her, she was about to go to Delhi. She won't get out of my jeep, she's afraid to see her parents." Sam went outside and returned with Amla. When Amla saw her father she fell on the floor crying. Ramesh held her in his arms.

"We should let the others know or they'll be up all night."

"I'll do it." Sam ran ahead of Prem, into the dining room. "Prem found Amla at the Haridwar train station. She was on her way to Delhi."

"Thank God!" Serena broke into sobs, Alicia hugged her.

"Well, that's a relief." Lucy yawned. "My intuition told me she was safe and we'd soon get her back."

Sam glared hatefully at Lucy. "You owe Amla an apology. It was sheer luck that Prem saw her on the railway platform. God knows what would've happened to her. When village girls like Amla go to the city they're forced into prostitution or they're raped and killed. It's your fault, you accused her of stealing, which was why she ran away."

"It was a perfectly logical conclusion. I saw Serena's chain around her neck."

"Serena gave it to her."

"That was a superior gesture on Serena's part, nevertheless, whether Amla is responsible or not, my necklace is still missing."

"You assume that because someone is poor, he is, by nature, a thief? Or that servants don't deserve apologies because they're servants?"

"No, I do not! You think that people with money don't have any feelings or morals!"

"Don't you tell me what I think about anything."

"Then don't lecture me about what it means to have money and how I should feel sorry for all the suffering people in the world and give it all away! I can smell your sort a mile off, you creep up on me, waiting for the right moment to pull out your little grant proposal or tell me about your charity hospital. It's my business what I do with my money, not yours!"

"I don't give a damn what you do with your money. You owe Amla an apology!"

"Someone took my necklace and I want it back!" Lucy hurled her chair against the wall.

"I'm going to talk to Masterji." Sam grabbed Jodi's flashlight and went out of the door.

Masterji called Jodi, Ramesh, Shanti and Amla to his cottage at eight in the morning. Prem sent word to Lucy that her private audience was scheduled for the coming Saturday.

Ramesh and Shanti arranged Amla's marriage within three days. They found a boy, Ramu, whose father was the *chowkidar* at the Kailash Dry Goods Exchange. On Friday afternoon Amla and Ramu were married in Jodi and Anu's garden. Anu set up a *shamiana* in the rose arbor and Ramesh hired three assistant cooks for the feast. George and Serena gave the couple a set of cooking pots, Sam painted a watercolour portrait of Shanti and Ramesh, Sanjal gave a gold-plated bangle, Dipali donated a red silk sari which Amla wore for the ceremony. Ramu wore a new white suit and gold turban, Ramesh borrowed Prem's silk jacket. Masterji performed the ceremony with the local pandit, Baja's supplied a band and a horse for the groom. The sun came out around mid-morning and stayed out for the rest of the day. Rain fell at dusk, then the sun reappeared and a faint rainbow appeared over the valley.

Amla wept miserably to leave her parents, though it was only a twenty-minute walk to Ramu's house. After Ramu and Amla said goodbye and started down the hill, Shanti and her remaining five daughters clung to Sam and sobbed.

Lucy left a wedding present for the newlyweds with Anu—an antique silver necklace she'd purchased at the Oberoi on her way through Delhi—and two hundred American dollars inside one of her personalised note cards.

"My sister is a completely selfish creature." Sanjal's hair was in its usual late evening disarray: there were oil spots on her purple silk shirt, her make-up was melting into her cheeks. "She never consults anyone on her schedule, she does exactly what she likes. Now I'm stranded with half my clothes gone in her luggage."

"What's happened?" Jodi knew exactly what had happened. Don and Dipali and Dipali's retinue left the morning after the wedding without telling anyone but the Khannas. The ostensible reasons were Don's meetings in Bombay and Dipali's cousin's wedding in Poona. For three hours Jodi had been waiting for Sanjal to come into his room for alcohol and sympathy. She had insulted him and this was his opportunity for revenge.

"Is your sister carrying on with that Don character?"

"My sister feels that she should be the center of attention at all times because she's the maharani. I pity her really, she's so out of touch." Jodi handed Sanjal a drink, which she swallowed whole. He sat back on the couch, arms crossed behind his head.

"What's the matter with you Jodi?"

"I'm just listening." He refilled her glass.

"I've got to see Masterji again. I can tell I'm about to enter a crisis. I have to talk to him tomorrow if possible." She lay her head on his shoulder. "I don't know why I don't just move here. Just looking at Masterji makes me feel calm."

"He is a fine fellow to spend time with, that I know." Jodi settled one hand on her shoulder, the other on her leg.

"You're so lucky to live near him."

"Indeed I am." Jodi turned off the light. He felt Sanjal's moist breath on his neck, her hair on his hands, and shuddered with revulsion.

Lucy paused every other minute to check her make-up and hair in her pocket mirror. Finally Prem summoned her into Masterji's room. Masterji's face, his white shawl and his hands seemed to glow in the half light.

"So Masterji, have you decided?"

"Decided?"

"About, about who gets initiated, I mean, isn't that what we've all been waiting for?"

"Ah yes—no I haven't. But that shouldn't matter to you."

Lucy shifted in her chair. "So—so that's it?"

"Tell me Lucy, what do you want?"

"What do I want?"

"Yes. What do you really want?"

"Oh, I—I—" Lucy gazed into Masterji's silver-blue eyes which bathed her in their healing light, and felt torrents of need and shame swell in her chest. She knew what she really wanted, but she couldn't say it, couldn't admit that she wanted to be beautiful, loved, admired and sought after, like Alicia.

"You want recognition and admiration, don't you?"

"Well, yes, doesn't everyone? You've got it, everyone else has got it. I've tried, Masterji, truly I have, you don't know how I've tried to make sense of my life. But I've never known what to do with myself. I've done everything all wrong, I know it, no one's ever told me how to behave . . . I should just give it all up and move into an *ashram*." Tears ran down Lucy's cheeks, carrying loose particles of mascara. She quickly wiped them off and blew her nose into a pink handkerchief. "I want someone to listen to me for once! I want someone to pay attention!"

"You have a large house in London. The lady who runs my London institute is looking for a building for a homeless shelter. Perhaps you could help her in some way."

"Masterji, I'd be thrilled, utterly thrilled to help her! My house is just sitting there, Lord knows I only use it half the year. Oh Masterji, what a wonderful, perfect idea!"

"There is going to be a meeting in Delhi in two weeks with the people who run my worldwide organisations. You should attend it."

"I'm already thinking of events and things to plan, oh Masterji, you really are a saint!" Lucy kissed Masterji on both cheeks.

Anu felt that she had sufficiently discharged her hostessing duties and stopped having dinner parties. The guests ate in their rooms or at separate tables in the rose arbor. George took a vow of silence and withdrew to his room. Serena ventured out only to ask for food or to hand over her laundry.

In the evening Alicia walked to the Shiva temple where she could see the Ganges. The sky throbbed with light, it was so active, so alive compared to the sky in America, which was dulled by pollution and neon lights and pushed so far out of reach that it no longer mingled with human life. The moon dangled just above the horizon, throwing a jagged light across the river. It resembled a woman's tresses lain across a man's torso, like the calendar poster at the Kailash Dry Goods Emporium of the Goddess Ganga lying over Shiva's forehead and shoulders. She wanted to lie down and sleep, her head hurt, her brain seemed to swell, to absorb all the dirt and noise and vapours in the atmosphere. She heard footsteps on dead leaves, she looked around, afraid, but it was only Shanti's nephew, the one whose father had run off to America. They nodded, he lit a cigarette and squatted on a rock, his body eclipsed the line of moonlight that cut across the water. He looked like a child of twelve, his eyes fixed in a perpetual daydream, his moustache just a faint line above his soft lips, a tattered red jacket, a 007 belt holding up thin trousers that were frayed at the bottom and had a torn inseam. She wondered how old he was, if he was married and had a child, or several children living in one of the huts on the mountainside. He offered her a cigarette, she reached forward, and saw his expression when he noticed the size of her gold bracelets. She pulled back so her sleeve would cover them. She smiled weakly, he blushed and looked away.

They sat together for several minutes, smoking and staring at the river. Alicia became acutely aware of his worn shoes and torn pants, that one of her gold bracelets could buy his entire family, and Shanti's family a house with a tin roof and a concrete floor. She didn't want to insult him by giving him her bracelet or some money, she couldn't talk to him in his language, she felt stupid nodding and smiling and pretending that there really wasn't any difference between his life and hers.

She stood up and waved goodbye, he waved back, smiling gently. She walked through the arbor to Prem's room. The light was off and the door padlocked from outside. She was angry that he wasn't there, or hadn't invited her to have dinner with him or go wherever he'd gone. Small clouds of smoke floated from the chimney of Masterji's cottage. She wanted to pound on the door and wake Masterji and make him explain himself. If he wasn't going to transform her or choose her, he should at least help her find what she so desperately sought, or he should touch her forehead and give her the *shaktipat*, or some kind of sign that she had come here for a reason. She was angry with him for acting as a teacher and not as a shaman. She clasped the door handle, she wanted to open it, but she couldn't. She ran back to the guest house and crouched on the porch. She thought of Shanti's nephew, she couldn't dispel the images of his James Bond belt buckle, his face wrenched with the anguish of never having had enough of food or clothing or attention. She had the luxury to ruminate over how and where to spend her money, to wonder who in her circle of acquaintances was deceitful. She wondered if what Masterji said was true, "from all desire comes lamenting, give up desire and you shall give up lamenting . . ."

Alicia dreamt that Masterji led her down a long corridor to a white room. She sat on a bed while he kissed her hands and placed his head on her lap. She awoke when it was still dark, she looked over her boots and clothes and books, all the things she had collected in defense and indulgence. Everything was submerged in night, sleep and death—the whole effort had failed. There was no man, no lover or teacher; Masterji was in his cottage, her father had left years ago. But somehow it did not matter. She felt strangely calm, she understood for the first time, the overwhelming power of Masterji's detachment, that there was no need to assign, to blame, or to struggle. At some point in the black hollow of the early morning, she had surrendered her quest.

"Hello, Sam!" Masterji struggled to his feet and squeezed Sam's hand affectionately.

"I've brought this for you." She handed him a large package. He opened the paper and delicately pulled out a watercolour painting of his cottage and the surrounding orchard.

"Did you paint this?"

"Yes." Sam bowed her head and blushed.

"Oh my—how beautiful your work is—beautiful—such patience you have—yes—there it is, my little cottage . . ." He studied the picture for several minutes, then settled it on the side-table, under the lamp. "How kind of you to give me such a gift."

"I just want to thank you for inviting me to the teachings."

"So, Sam . . ." He stared at her, with infinite kindness. She looked like an orphan in her tattered sweater, bits of ragged hair extruding from holes in her Kulu hat, her dark, solemn eyes afraid to ask for help. "So, I've been thinking of what you should do. You should go back to America and become a teacher."

Sam started to cry. "Please don't send me away, Masterji, please. I can't live anywhere else but in India. I can't, this is the only place I can live in. Please don't send me away, not again, please."

"There, there . . ." He took her hands and pressed them between his palms.

"Can't you do something, anything? I'll do whatever you want, anything." Sam bent over and sobbed. Masterji patted her shoulder until her voice wore itself out from crying. She wiped her face on her shirt sleeves and took several deep, steadying breaths.

"We need people to help run the orphanage. We need good teachers. We have so many children who need to learn to read. You should be one of our teachers. You can live in the room next to Prem." Sam listened, and felt, to her amazement, the heavy bonds of frustration and fear dissolve in her heart. She wondered why this idea hadn't occured to her years ago. Masterji had just given her a vocation that would bring satisfaction to herself and to everyone she knew, and after a long exile she would return to the sublime, brilliant world of her childhood.

"I can stay here?"

"Yes. You can help run the school. You'll be an excellent teacher. I remember you when you were a child, you were so gifted, you were an inspiration to all of us. Go talk to Prem." Sam fell on her knees and clutched his hand. "Go on, talk to Prem. I believe there's a nice room for you, bigger than the one you've got now. Go on, go see him now." Sam backed out of the room, gazing, in amazement, at Masterji.

Prem stood at his desk, sorting through the mail. Two boys sat in the corner with a composition book and a Hindi-English dictionary.

"Ah, you're here! I want to show you your room." Prem led Sam through the back of the compound to a square, sun-filled room beside the vegetable garden. It had a bed, a desk, a Tibetan carpet and a painting of Krishna dancing with cows.

"Do you need help moving in?"

"I don't think so."

"Look!"

A crane floated on the wind and dipped into the arbor.

"Beautiful."

"Yes."

Their hands touched. Prem smiled, she smiled back.

"I'm sorry you're leaving us so soon." Anu stood in the doorway and studied Lucy's room, every inch of which was covered with scarves, shawls, boots, face-creams, hats, books, sunglasses.

"Well, I know, it's a heartbreak after all the fun we've had, but just got a telegram from my friend Victor insisting that I join him for a special meeting in Italy with all these divine people in the environmental movement. It's a two-week retreat on a mountain-top chateau, everyone's going to get up at dawn and pray together and then talk about how we can all save the earth. I've learned never to say No to Victor, after all, he introduced me to Masterji in the first place. Anu darling, can you see if the taxi's come? And tell Sanjal to hurry up."

"So you won't be attending the conference in Delhi for Masterji's charities?" Anu eyed the cashmere sweaters, silks scarves and the silver fox coat thrust casually into one of the bronze leather suitcases.

"I would adore to, but this really is a once-in-a-lifetime thing. Masterji will understand, I'm doing something so much more important, after all, without clean air and water and food, one can't even think about meditating and doing one's yoga and building shelters for the homeless, right?"

"That's a point. Your car has come." Ramesh and Gobind carried Lucy's luggage down the stairs. Lucy and Sanjal gave

Anu numerous hugs and kisses and got into the taxi. Ramesh and Shanti and their remaining five daughters waved goodbye from the gate as the taxi started down the hillside.

Anu went back into the house to make sure the beds were being stripped. Shanti found a red leather jacket in Sanjal's closet which she gave to Anu. Anu took it back to the main house to store in the Lost and Found trunk. She felt something hard in one of the pockets of the jacket, reached in and found Lucy's gold necklace with the three blue sapphires, which Sanjal had borrowed and forgotten.

Alicia made her reservation for the Delhi train. She gave her clothes to Amla's sisters, her camera to Sam, $200,000 to the school and orphanage, her boots, jacket and leather knapsack to Shanti and all of her jewellery to Shanti's cousins.

George, Serena and Jodi joined Alicia for a farewell breakfast. Alicia drank her final cup of tea, hoisted her bag over her shoulder and went to the front desk to call a taxi. Shanti waved her towards Masterji's cottage. Alicia hadn't said goodbye to Masterji, she'd written a short note, she knew that he wasn't well and didn't want to bother him. Shanti pulled Alicia's sleeve, Alicia left her bag by the desk and followed Shanti to the cottage. She went down the hallway to Masterji's room. Masterji sat in his chair—a book, a scarf and a rose bouquet on his lap. Masterji did not speak, he simply stared at her. Her heart beat wildly, she fumbled for something to say.

"I heard you weren't well, so I didn't want to bother you before I left."

"I wanted to talk to you. You've changed very much since the teachings."

"I have?"

"Yes. More than anyone else."

"In what way?"

"You've allowed the teachings to penetrate you." He gathered the book, the scarf and the rose and held them out. "Here, Alicia, these are yours."

"What for?"

"Yes, my dear, yes . . ."

"It's, it's—not . . ."

"Yes. I've chosen you."

She fell on her knees and pressed her forehead against his feet.

Serena paced around Anu's garden while George had his final audience in Masterji's cottage. Forty minutes passed, became an hour. She began to panic. She wanted to get out of Devigunj, out of India. If George wanted to stay she would go without him. After two hours Masterji's door creaked open. Prem waved to Serena; she buttoned her jacket and followed Prem to Masterji's room. Prem closed the door, George wasn't there, she was alone with Masterji.

For several minutes Masterji sat slumped in his chair. Serena was about to leave when he lifted his head.

"I'm glad you came."

"You are?"

"I think you will stay here in India for a while."

Serena frowned. Masterji stared at her, then placed his right hand on her forehead. Suddenly she felt the force of thousands and thousands of lights explode in her brain. She didn't know how long he left his hand on her forehead, whether it was a few seconds or many hours. When he removed his hand everything in the room settled into its familiar shape and colour, but nothing had any solid mass—it was a swarm of vibrating particles. He sat as before, slumped in his large velvet chair, the white shawl around his shoulders and knees. She stood without feeling the floor or the currents of cold air streaming through the window and the cracks in the walls. She moved down the hall and out into the garden, where everything spun about in waves of multicoloured light; she didn't know if she was standing or floating or lying on the earth.

"Serena! Serena darling!" George seized her shoulders. "Serena, I want to get married, right away. That's what I want, may be Masterji would do it for us. Oh darling!" He kissed her mouth and cheeks and forehead, but she didn't feel anything.

"Don't . . ." She pushed him away.

"Serena, are you alright?"

"Don't touch me." She lay on the grass, the sky throbbed with billions of radiant pulses of colour, she felt herself merging with all the heat and light in the air.

Masterji watched as the sun slid below the rim of the mountain, drenching the clouds with its golden colour, then raised a cigarette to his lips, inhaled and sighed.

In the Heart of Braj

LILA FIRST MET SHYAM SUNDER IN NEW DELHI while renewing her Indian visa. Lila's uncle worked at the American Embassy and Shyam Sunder was from a political family, so a duty officer from the embassy was assigned to take them down to the External Affairs office to facilitate their path through the Indian bureaucracy. The consular officer who met her said that Shyam Sunder, whom he called "the Whitmore kid", was "richer than hell . . . he's doing some kind of research near Agra." When a young man with a shaved head wearing a saffron dhoti and *tulsi* beads around his neck and wrists introduced himself as Shyam Sunder, the officer was aghast, and quickly steered Lila into an embassy car. When Shyam Sunder produced his American passport, the officer allowed him to sit in the front with the Indian driver.

Mr Ramaswami and Mr Mehrotra, the department heads in the visa section, knew Shyam Sunder very well. He'd been in India for eight years and had therefore renewed his visa sixteen times. Lila and Shyam Sunder were moved to the front of the line, two boys were dispatched for tea and *rasgullahs*. Shyam Sunder spent fifteen minutes discussing Tamil Shaivite poetry with Mr Ramaswami, who was from Madras, while the passports were passed through the office to be wondrously held and studied. Shyam Sunder quoted a line from Kabir and was rewarded with a collective swaying of heads and clucking of tongues. A Frenchman who complained about the favouritism shown to Shyam Sunder and Lila, was put in the back of the line and made to wait an extra hour.

The embassy officer twitched miserably in his seersucker suit. He whispered to Lila that the tea was unsanitary and speculated as to how long Shyam Sunder planned to spend prattling on about poetry with the clerks, he had a lunch date back at the American club. After forty minutes, Mr Ramaswami and Mr Mehrotra stamped and signed visa extensions in both the passports and assured Lila and Shyam Sunder that they had both been Indians in their past lives, while all the peons and tea bearers gazed from halls and doorways and the embassy officer fled down the stairs. As Lila was about to step into a scooter, Shyam Sunder handed her a slip of paper with his address and invited her to visit him in Brindavan.

A week later, Lila got off the bus at Mathura. She was exhausted. Dust and perspiration clung to her, covering her skin in a dirty paste. She had no idea where she was or how to find Shyam Sunder. A small boy led her to a slightly older boy who lay stretched out across a rickshaw, smoking a *bidi*. When Lila said Brindavan, he shook his head. When she offered more money, he slowly roused himself and pulled the rickshaw towards the road. His thin legs trembled as he pushed down the bicycle pedals, joining the line of bicycle traffic that moved towards the horizon, where a vermilion disc of sun tinted the forest pink and gold.

It was dark when she found Shyam Sunder's house. Above the door there were three signs in Hindi, Bengali and English, which read: "Bhakti Prem Institute of Devotional Studies, Vallabhacharya Sampradaya, Vrindavan, Braj District,

U.P. India." A chowkidar unbolted the door and Lila asked for Shyam Sunder. He grunted and led her into the courtyard. Two women scowled from the stairs, an old man belched and chewed *paan* in a doorway. After fifteen minutes Shyam Sunder leaned over the balcony and waved Lila upstairs, into his room.

"Sit, sit! How did you come?"

"I took the bus from Delhi to Mathura and a rickshaw from there."

"That's a long way on a rickshaw."

"I had a nice driver. He told me to ask for him when I go back, his name is Madan Mohan."

"That means 'beguiler of the mind and heart!'" Shyam Sunder laughed and rocked backwards. "Everyone in Braj is named for Krishna."

"What does your name mean?"

"The beautiful dark one." He blushed, and abruptly stood up, his left hand tight around his prayer necklace. He was an extremely handsome, extremely intense young man. He had unusually brilliant, pale blue eyes, pink and white skin and light brown hair which was shaved except for a long tassel which ran down his back in the Vaishnavite fashion. He radiated a powerful, nearly visible aura. Lila was wary of coming too close to him.

"I have to go to bed, I get up at four for prayers. Your room's here." Shyam Sunder led Lila down the hall to a small room with bright green walls, a bed, a single light bulb suspended from the ceiling and an out-of-date calendar from Jagdish Motors. The chowkidar wheezed and glared as he hauled the last of Lila's bags upstairs. She had too much luggage, she realised, and far too many books, including an enormous Hindi-English Dictionary and a hard-bound double edition of the Oxford History of India. The chowkidar scowled at her, she stared back impassively. She did not feel compelled to tip someone who was supposed to be part of a religious organisation. But when it was clear that he had no intention of leaving unless he got a tip, she gave him five rupees, which he examined for tears and scotch tape and then stuck into his dhoti.

Lila itched from dirt and sweat, but there was no place to shower, there wasn't even a faucet, only a small jar of gray water on the side-table. She was suddenly angry to have spent two and a half hours on a dirty bus and another two and a half hours on a bicycle rickshaw and then be denied a shower and a cold drink. She wiped her hands and feet on one of her shirts and lay over the rigid mattress. She could hear chants and drums from temples, moans of cows and dogs from the street . . . the air smelled of dung and decaying flowers. She wondered if she'd made a mistake to come to this strange place, to impose on this man she hardly knew, though it was the sort of place where she could isolate herself from people and the compulsion to talk to them which was what she really wanted from India. But all she'd done in the months she'd spent in Delhi was go to weddings and embassy receptions and textile exhibitions.

The next morning, Lila tapped on the door of Shyam Sunder's study; he sat cross-legged before a small writing desk in a bright orange kurta which enhanced the whiteness of his skin and the vivid blueness of his eyes. His tassle of brown hair was combed into a small braid, his whole person exuded precision and order. In the morning light she could see how organised and clean the room was, from the books that lined the walls to the stacked bamboo mats and the shrine in the corner. He smiled when he saw her and poured her a cup of coffee from a thermos.

"Did you sleep alright?"

"Yes, thanks," Lila lied, carefully.

"Would it be alright with you if I work in the mornings and take you around in the afternoons?"

"If it's not any trouble . . ."

'No, no, I enjoy revisiting all the sites, it's the easiest way to accumulate merit, that's why everyone does it." He opened his desk and took out a Hindi manuscript and a tape-recorder. Lila scanned the bookshelves and saw, among volumes of Hindi, Bengali, Sanskrit and English literature, several rows of French and Italian novels with cracked and faded spines, an indication that they had once been penetrated and explored.

"Where did you get those novels?"

"Those? In college I majored in Romance Languages. I wanted to live in Rome."

"What made you come to India?"

"My mother was trying to get me out of what she regarded an ill-considered love affair. She sent me here for a four-week holiday with some friends who were living in Delhi. We went to the Taj Mahal; I was walking through the Agra bazaar when I saw two men squatting and smoking a *chillum,* and right away, something flashed in my head—it all looked totally familiar. I felt something pulling me in another direction, I started walking and saw my guru sitting in a *chi* stall. He asked me to come to Brindavan, I followed him that afternoon. Three days later I took my vows and became his disciple."

"What did your parents think?"

"They tried to have me kidnapped, they tried to bribe my guru and all the local officials. My mother set up camp at a hotel in Agra and told me she'd kill herself if I didn't come home."

"Did —"

"No no, she didn't, it was just a threat, she's not the type of person who'd willingly get out of anyone's way." He took an anxious breath, as if the episode had just transpired, or was about to happen again. "My guru said Krishna protected me. If you come next year, then you can meet him. He's gone to Puri now. That's his picture." He pointed to a grainy black and white photograph of a man with ferocious eyes, long black hair and beard. Lila glanced from the photograph to Shyam Sunder, wondering how he could have fallen under the spell of the peculiar, intimidating face of the guru. She was glad he wasn't there, she knew she did not want to meet him, or observe his effect on Shyam Sunder.

In the afternoons, Shyam Sunder and Lila visited the pilgrimage sites in Braj, the towns, the sacred ponds and gardens, the temples and ashrams along the Jumna. The dust and moisture seemed to seep into her skin and hair—it wouldn't come out, no matter how often she washed. She didn't like taking her shoes off at the temples, the floors were covered with sour milk and marigolds which stuck to her feet. And yet she felt there was something special about the place, she felt it at some of the temples and sacred ponds, she saw it in the faces of the pilgrims who came from every part of India—some from as far as Tamil Nadu and Kashmir—to pray for a son, a good rebirth, or just to pay homage to Krishna. They considered everything born in Braj, from mosquitoes to dogs to cows and Brahmins, to be the holiest beings in the universe because Krishna was born there. Some circumambulated the town fully prostrate, some taking one step at a time, some recited thousands of mantras or took vows of silence and long fasts which, Shyam Sunder said, brought infinitely greater merit when performed in the holy realm of Braj.

No one ever mistook Shyam Sunder for one of the Hare Krishnas; they ran a guest house on the other side of town and made occasional forays into the bazaar wearing badly wrapped dhotis and saris and attempting to speak Hindi. The swamis and students at the temples, the cooks and children at *chai* stalls—all knew Shyam Sunder. Lila was amazed at the way he spoke Hindi, and when he spoke

English, she could almost see, traced on his orange robes and shaved head, a young man with hair, holding a wine glass, feet in polished loafers, legs in white pants. He had retained many vestigal gestures of his New England origins: he opened doors for Lila and sometimes used a finger bowl after meals. But as she watched him laughing and joking among the *Brijvasis*, rocking on his haunches and moving his head from side to side, only his pale eyes and skin betrayed the fact that he wasn't born among them.

Lila wasn't sure how to behave around Shyam Sunder. If she made a random joke, he would either scowl or close his eyes and laugh and say, "Very good, very good." He described the bliss of spiritual ardour, of never wanting or needing anything but God, then he'd launch into a discourse on temple architecture or the Mughal postal system. He never asked personal questions, which was perplexing as they spent more time together. Whenever he entered a temple his mouth parted and his eyes shone with tears. When he spoke of Krishna, he blushed and melted into smiles like a woman. Lila kept a respectful distance from Shyam Sunder when they visited temples; sometimes she laid flowers before an idol, hoping to win his approval.

Soon it became too hot to sleep indoors, so everyone in the institute slept on the roof. Lila often lay awake, listening to birds and insects hissing in the garden, listening to human voices animals crying, or a chowkidar whistling, or sounds she couldn't identify. She stared across at the other roofs, where people lay shrouded under sheets and mosquito nets, or she stared into the sky until the stars receded and an orange light spread over the clouds and bird sounds swelled on the light.

One morning, when everyone was out, Lila went into Shyam Sunder's room. All the manuscripts were in their place, the prayer beads in neat rows, the mats stacked in the corner. She pulled out a cloth-bound photo album and opened to a page of photographs of a summer birthday party on the lawn of a colonial mansion. There were several pictures of a severe, attractive blonde woman, who appeared to be Shyam Sunder's mother, opening presents, toasting herself with a champagne glass, her arms protectively around Shyam Sunder's shoulders. He was amazingly handsome, with the same brilliantly clear eyes, but with thick light brown hair skimming his shoulders. His mother fixed voracious, adoring eyes on him as he played a flute and posed with a tennis racket. There were more photographs of sleek, tanned adults around buffet tables with dogs and children underfoot. At the back of the album, there was a picture of Shyam Sunder in academic robes accepting a plaque with a clipping that read: "David Whitmore, age 16, wins Latin Prize for composition." On the following page Shyam Sunder sat with his arms around a pretty brunette. Lila felt a wild surge of jealousy towards the girl who might have been a cousin or a sister, but could also have been a girlfriend. She reached for another album when she heard voices in the courtyard. Shoving the books back into the shelf, she ran down the hall and into her room, her heart pounding with guilt and excitement. Shyam Sunder put his head through the door.

"Had lunch?"

"No."

"I want to show you something." He started down the hall, she glanced in her mirror and ran after him.

They drove to a pond called Radha Kunj which, Shyam Sunder said, was made from the tears that Radha shed when Krishna left Braj. They ate lunch on an old pavilion and lay down in the shade. Shyam Sunder fell asleep, his mouth settled into a beautiful smile. Lila could see the lines of his arms and legs through his saffron clothes. He had to have made love to someone back in America . . . it wasn't possible for a man so handsome to go through life without having attempted to fall in love. She wondered how he could be celibate when he worshipped a god who was so unashamedly erotic. All the temples showed Krishna embracing women, all the songs were about arousal, jealousy, satisfaction, desire. She thought of the girl in the photograph, his reference to an ill-considered affair. Shyam Sunder opened his eyes, she yawned to pretend she'd just woken up.

"How long have we been here?"

"I don't know."

"I'd guess about two hours." He stared at two huge turtles hovering around a lotus pad. "Do you plan to get married, Lila?"

"Not right now, I'm only twenty."

"But you expect that you will?"

"Well, yes, didn't you, once?"

"May be. But there's no point in it."

"Why not?"

"It can only last a few years at best. And eventually we all separate when we die, so why bother?" Shyam Sunder stood on one of the sandstone pavilions and threw the remains of his lunch to the fish. A funeral raft drifted along the current. Lila saw something moving on the water by the far bank, long and black, bobbing up and down on the current. It came closer. She saw two round spheres, an elbow and a foot. It was a human body. More turtles swam after it, in a moment it was just a whirlpool on the water's surface. The current moved the raft out of sight, Shyam Sunder stared at the water till it ran smooth.

Suddenly the sky went orange and they were caught in a dust storm. They leaned against a tree and pressed their palms over their faces. The wind passed, Lila opened her eyes and saw a grove of huge trees upon the horizon.

"This place feels haunted."

"It is. It's where Krishna danced the Rasa Lila."

The wind stung them, they pressed their faces into their sleeves. Lila clutched Shyam Sunder's arm to keep from falling over.

"Are you alright?"

"Yes, it's just—so beautiful . . ."

"I know." Their hands touched, the wind jostled them apart.

That evening, Shyam Sunder didn't play his harmonium or read his poetry translations on the roof as he usually did. He sat very still, his chin on his knees. Lila yearned to talk to him. After forty minutes she drew courage and spoke.

"Are you happy living here?"

"Happy?" Shyam Sunder frowned. "I don't know anyone who is happier than I am. I suppose I could be back in America living off my family's money, but I wouldn't necessarily be happier there. I'm in full control of my life and my time now. But I don't want to proselytise my path, I've had a hard enough time defending it to the people I grew up with."

"Don't they accept it now?"

"Yes, but they consider me a failure. They think my brother is a success because he works in a law firm and wants to enter politics like my father. It doesn't matter that he's a big game hunter, or that he abandoned his wife and children and reviles anything to do with religion, probably because of me. If I'd stayed in America and lived off my trust fund, I'd probably be a professor or an art collector, or a great reader of books and a writer of letters. But where would I be in my next life? I'd have used all my good karma without expelling karmas from my past lives that have not yet ripened and I'd probably make a lot of new karma that I would have to work off in many future lives. Think of all the animals my brother's killed, what that will mean for him . . . . Now I have a human body, which takes 8,400,000 rebirths in lower-life forms to attain. I can use the moment of death to be free from endless rebirths, but if I don't, I'll endure another rebirth, and another."

Lila didn't understand what his past and future lives had to do with her question. "But what do you have here that's—that you can't find elsewhere?"

"It's impossible to describe what happens when the veil is lifted." His eyelids fluttered, he smiled wondrously. Lila frowned. "The *Brijvasis* say that sometimes Krishna grants certain people a favour by lifting the veil of Maya, and for an instant they see everything as an illusion. I can't describe what it's like . . . by the way, where did you get your name?"

"I was told it belonged to a character in a fairy tale."

"You know what it means in Sanskrit, don't you?"

"No."

"Lila is the cosmic play of the Gods. They create this universe for their pleasure and dissolve it when it no longer interests them."

"I'm not sure I like that."

"No, no, it's beautiful." He brushed his hands against her cheek. She shuddered, as if he'd kissed every part of her body.

Lila lay awake on her charpoy that night listening to the drone of drums and voices of two men in the temple sustaining their chant through the night. She wanted Shyam Sunder to hold her. It was impossible—he was a monk, yet she was tormented by hope. When she was alone, she could think of nothing but his face and words; when they were together she could barely meet his eyes or answer when he spoke to her.

In the morning she walked to the river and sat on one of the dilapidated ghats. The sun blazed over the sand, three women pounded their laundry on the rocks. They sang as they worked, rinsing, pounding, laying orange and blue clothes flat to dry. It was a reassuring scene, the diurnal rituals of ordinary life, enacted and sustained, but it made Lila miserable. Shyam Sunder's detachment wounded her, she didn't want to be detached from life, she wanted to taste and touch everything around her. Tears rose in her eyes, she pressed her face into her hands and wondered why, in this most sensual of places, one was taught to turn away from sense.

When she returned to the institute, Shyam Sunder was waiting in the courtyard. He smiled and handed her two saris.

"I just bought these for you in the bazaar. Try them on."

She blushed violently and glanced in shame at her shirt. "I'm sorry, I didn't..."

"I just thought you'd look nice in them." Lila unfolded the saris. They were blue and white weaves, very simple and elegant, like Shyam Sunder. "I don't know your size so I couldn't get a choli, but Madan's daughter said she'd lend you one." The girl led Lila upstairs, dressed her in one of the saris, pushed glass bangles over her wrists and put a *bindi* on her forehead.

"How does it feel?" Shyam Sunder peered through the door.

"It's—it's nice."

"Today there's a celebration for Vishnu's fourth incarnation, Narasimha, the Man-Lion. We're going to the Banke Bihari temple. The midday *darshan* ends at 12.30. Don't take your camera, they don't allow photographs."

Lila followed Shyam Sunder through the bazaar to an alley lined with widows and cripples begging for alms. At the end of the alley, a blind man leaned on a staff chanting "Radhe Radhe Govinda Govinda Radhe..." Lila dropped ten rupees in his hand. Without breaking his chant, he gave a nod and tucked the note into his shirt. Shyam Sunder and Lila bought several garlands of roses and jasmine, left their chappals with a chowkidar and stepped through the door. Lila's nostrils filled with the odour of marigolds and sour milk—the perfume of Hindu temples. Shyam Sunder went to the men's section and bowed before the idol. Lila pulled her sari over her head and went to the women's section. The idol was three-feet high, carved in black stone and dressed in white silk and gold ornaments; its legs were crossed, it played on a flute. Everyone sang *Hari Bol*, hands stretched up, the priests doused the crowd with water and milk. Lila followed the line of women that went forward to touch the marble wall that supported the deity. Suddenly she felt wildly giddy, she started laughing uncontrollably. Milk and water lashed her face, two women seized her forearm and shook her so hard she fainted. When she opened her eyes she saw a circle of women standing over her, pointing and laughing. The idol was shut away behind heavy silver doors, people were filing out of the temple. Lila pushed her sari into place and went outside. Shyam Sunder was waiting with her chappals. Lila tried to keep from laughing, he looked so peculiar with his white skin and orange dhoti, holding the shoes in one hand and his prayer beads in another.

"The idol here is Banke Bihari Krishna as a young man, a teenager, actually."

"Really?" she giggled wildly into her forearms. He began to laugh.

"This was the first place I visited when I came to Brindavan. I had quite a reaction to it also. Come on." They walked single file through the bazaar to the institute and had an enormous meal with all the students and their families. The children performed a play in the courtyard. At dusk they went up to the roof to sing *bhajans* with Madan. Lila imagined that she would stay in Brindavan, that she and Shyam Sunder would live together; he sang so beautifully, and smiled when she tried to sing along with him. At midnight Shyam Sunder closed the harmonium and Madan tied a cloth over his tabla. They pulled their mats onto the roof, Lila didn't join the women, she lay beside Shyam Sunder, who fell asleep with the same serene smile she had seen that afternoon at Radha Kunj.

When Lila awoke she put on her new sari, combed her hair and went to Shyam Sunder's study. It was empty, the kitchen and the courtyard were empty, everyone was gone except for the two old men who sat chanting in the prayer room. Two hours later she heard footsteps. She ran to Shyam Sunder's room and saw him packing a suitcase.

"What happened?"

"I just got a telegram from America. My mother's had a heart attack. She wants to see me, I have to leave right away." His face was strained, the muscles in his arms tightened as he pushed his books into the suitcase and bent to fold his kurtas and dhotis into neat rectangles.

"When was the last time you saw her?"

"Five years ago. She came here to make one last effort to get me to leave. She wouldn't come here so I met her at the Clark Shiraz in Agra, the five-star hotel she always stayed in. She cried when she saw me, she gave me a plane ticket and an envelope with thousands of dollars in it, she offered to buy me a town house in New York if I came home."

"Why didn't you go?"

"I didn't have a choice. My whole life is here." He stopped folding clothes and stared at the picture of his guru, then sat on the bed and dropped his head in his hands. Lila sat beside him. She wanted to cry, she couldn't believe that he was leaving.

"She'll be happy to see you."

"If she's still alive when I get there. I wish she could've believed that my life here is not a—a waste, as she kept saying. I wasn't escaping from a bad life, I had an extraordinary life. But the moment I saw my guru I . . . it was . . . I knew I had to . . ." He covered his face and cried. Lila touched his shoulder. He looked up at her, she tried to pour all the feeling she had for him into her gaze. Their knees and elbows touched, he turned away to wipe his face and shifted a half inch further away from her, then quickly stood.

"You can stay as long as you like. We're all very fond of you here."

Lila swallowed hard—it was the first time he had ever expressed any kind of feeling for her.

"I can imagine what my family will say when they see me, I haven't been out of India for eight years." They both looked at his worn rubber chappals, his saffron dhoti and the *tulsi* beads around his neck and wrists. Lila ran to her room and brought back a green trench coat. He tried it on, it was tight around his shoulders but he blushed, he seemed grateful to have it.

"This is for you." He handed her a package wrapped in gold tinsel. The taxi horn bleated, the chowkidar called. They faced each other for a moment, he saluted and left. Everyone gathered in the courtyard to see him off. The women sobbed into their saris, the children cried, "Okay, bye-bye." Lila saw his brown tassle of hair slide behind the back window and his pale hand wave a general farewell as the taxi pulled away in a ball of dust. She ran to her room and opened her gift. It was two books: *The Gospel of Selfless Action or the Gita According to Gandhi* and *The Loves of Krishna, Bhakti Poetry* translated by W.G. Archer. She looked for inscriptions; in the *Gita* he had written, "For Lila, Best Regards, Shyam Sunder." In the other, "I have found a friend in the heart of Braj." She held the books against her heart and sobbed into her pillow.

For hours Lila didn't move. There were no sounds, no odours, all the rooms were shuttered against the sterile afternoon heat. She felt bitterly, horribly alone. Eventually the sky darkened. She felt the first cool flush of evening in the air, she heard shutters unlocking, cows and monkeys groaning for food, cymbals, drums, voices. She forced herself onto her feet, down the stairs, into the street. She walked through the lanes and roads and markets, till she came to the alley that led to the Banke Bihari temple. She dropped a coin into the palms of all the beggars, gave ten rupees to the blind man chanting Radhe Govind, bought a garland of roses and jasmine and went inside the temple. She inhaled the odour of milk and marigolds, she saw the priests flinging milk and water over the crowd. Suddenly she was overwhelmed by a dreadful, unbearable sadness. It was so much greater than what she had felt after Shyam Sunder left, it was like a huge river pouring over her, suffocating her. She dug her nails into her face and crawled over to the marble wall where women were sobbing and pounding their fists over their breasts and cheeks, she clung to the rail and screamed and beat her head against the wall until she lost consciousness.

When she opened her eyes she was lying beneath low clouds. Two women stood over her. She saw a gold swell on the horizon and a line of bathers by the river. It was morning, she was on a rooftop, next to Banke Bihari. Pigs and cows searched for food in the nullah; the ground was littered with wilted garlands, shreds of paper, banana peels. The women brought tea and bread. The sun turned white and the bathers disappeared from the river and Banke Bihari opened for morning darshan. Lila went into the bathroom, cleaned her arms, feet and face, arranged her sari, went down the stairs to the courtyard, bought a garland and went back into the temple.

She pushed her way to the front where the *pujaris* opened and closed the curtain. She stared at the black idol, dressed in gold and green, but she felt nothing. The crowd cried and swooned, she was sprayed with water, chants and bells pressed into her ears, but she felt nothing. She thrust towards the railing to hand her garland to a young priest. He was astonishingly beautiful. His eyes, hair, hands, arms and feet all shone with perfection. He dipped his index finger into a tin of red powder and asked her to come forward, but she couldn't move. He stared at her curiously, leaned over the railing and pressed his finger against her forehead. A swell of energy rose through her stomach, chest and throat and exploded in her head. She was suddenly oblivious to the heat and moisture and the crush of bodies around her; she blinked, and for an instant saw that everything was an illusion. Then came a piercing white light so powerful she thought her soul was about to depart from her body, whereupon she fainted.

The next day Lila went to the institute, took her bags and moved to the *dharamsala* next to Banke Bihari. She had to go to the temple every day and gaze at the young priest. She stood at the back to watch as he strolled back and forth, handing out food, flinging water and garlands over the crowd, chatting with the other priests, adjusting his lungi and stroking his hair. She didn't go near the front, she couldn't bring herself to speak to him. She woke up early in the mornings so she could go in before anyone else. She slept on the temple step in the afternoons so she could be the first for the evening darshan. Sometimes she fanned the idol while it rested in the afternoon, until an angry widow swatted her away and called her a dirty foreigner. She let the woman take over, she even left some food for her.

One day she went back to the *dharmasala* and found that all her things had been stolen: camera, typewriter, books, everything. She just laughed, she really didn't care. Once she was in such a hurry to get inside the temple she left her shoes on the front step, when she came out they were gone. The heat was ferocious, she walked barefoot over the stone pavement without minding the pain. When the reached the *dharamsala* she slid her silver bracelets off her wrists and gave them to a widow who was begging in the nullah.

Sometimes she found herself lying face down in a temple, or circumambulating a shrine, running her hand along the dirty line on the wall where hundreds of other hands had been, or kneeling into the Jumna water with thousands of people. Lila didn't know when she noticed that he noticed her, but one day he was staring at her as her gaze flickered from his eyes to the eyes of the idol. Then she saw him standing by the flower stalls watching her when she came out of the *dharamsala*. She thought he was following her through the bazaar. It seemed so dangerous to see him anywhere but the temple where there were lots of people around, she had no idea what she might do if he came onto the roof at night.

One afternoon she went to bathe in the river. The water stretched to the horizon where it dissolved in sunlight, the wind struck her in sharp piercing thrusts. She let herself into the water, letting it run into her eyes, her neck, her breasts. She wiped her face and arms and followed her footprints back towards the town. Her sari clung to her skin, making it hard to walk. She slipped, her sari caught in a thorn bush. She felt someone hovering about her. He was standing in the path, a damp lungi around his waist, his sacred thread across his torso. His hair stuck to his neck and shoulders, his arms were crossed across his chest, he tilted his head a little to one side, like the idol. He reached down and pulled the cloth off the thorn branch. When he stood up he was closer to her than before.

"Please come to my house for tea. Come this afternoon."

"Where is it?"

"Come to the temple, I'll tell you." She watched him toss rocks at his friends and disappear behind an old pavilion.

Lila didn't see him at the evening darshan. She wondered how she would find his house. She didn't sleep at all, she lay awake, running her hands over her arms and her breasts, wondering... In the morning she went to the temple but he wasn't there. She returned to the *dharamsala* at noon. The heat was ferocious. The two women were sleeping, all the doors and windows were shut. Lila rubbed sandal paste on her forehead and fanned herself with a palm leaf to cool the heat. She went downstairs and pushed the front door open. The street was deserted, there were no beggars, no monkeys or dogs picking at garbage, just heat and silence. She started walking. She came to a fork in the path and was about to step right when an impulse steered her left. An inner voice told her to turn back but she kept walking. Her feet moved faster, her sari fell off her shoulder. She heard someone whistle.

"Where're you going?" He was standing in a doorway.

"Just walking," she stammered, it didn't seem the right thing to say.

"Come in."

The inner voice screamed No but her feet moved dumbly after him. He led her to a small room next to a shuttered *chai* stall. The voice cried Don't go in, but she did. He told her to sit on a stool. Two boys watched from under a dirty curtain. She could smell the sandalwood oil on his body mixed with the musty squalor of the room. He took a tray and a brush, pulled another stool close to her, dipped the brush into a tin of white paint and touched it against her cheek. She flinched, he told her to keep still. He traced a line of dots around her cheeks and brow, it felt as if he was pushing his hands under her clothes. Five boys were now watching. She heard suppressed giggles and whispers, she felt the collective weight of many more eyes bearing down on her, yet she sat paralyzed on the stool as he continued. Every drop of paint felt like a needle piercing her skin. His hair fell over his brow and brushed her cheek, he stood back, tilted his head and smiled, then crouched closer. She was terrified that their bodies might touch and something really awful would happen. He put down the tray and handed her a mirror. She looked in the glass and saw a huge crowd pressing into the door, their eyes huge, mouths tight. He pointed and laughed, the boys screamed.